The Evil
in
Pemberley House

The Evil in Pemberley House

Philip José Farmer
and
Win Scott Eckert

SUBTERRANEAN PRESS 2009

For Bette

and Lisa:

Two of a Kind

WOLD NEWTON is a small village in the East Riding of Yorkshire County, England. It is chiefly famous for a meteorite which struck near it in 1795, the exact location of impact being marked by a monument which tourists, or anybody else, may see now. At the moment it struck, two large coaches with fourteen passengers and four coachmen were within a few yards of it. All were exposed to the ionization of the accompanying meteorites. The descendants of all those in or on the coaches include an extraordinary number of great crime fighters, scientists, and explorers. So many, in fact, that the only reasonable explanation is that the meteorite radiation caused a beneficial mutation of genes in those exposed.

The mutated genes were reinforced, kept from being lost, by the inbreeding of the descendants of those present at Wold Newton. Marriages of cousins were, of course, common among the British nobility and gentry… Moreover, most of the passengers came of stock which had been producing extraordinary men and women for many generations. Some of their descendants were more than extraordinary; they bordered on, and in some cases attained, the status of superman.

— "The Fabulous Family Tree of Doc Savage (Another Excursion into Creative Mythography)"
Doc Savage: His Apocalyptic Life, Philip José Farmer

"ARE THE shades of Pemberley to be thus polluted?"

— Lady Catherine de Bourgh to Elizabeth Bennet
Pride and Prejudice, Jane Austen

HOLMES SHOT out his long, thin arm and picked out Volume "H" in his encyclopaedia of reference. "'Holdernesse, 6th Duke, K.G., P.C.'—half the alphabet!...Married Edith, daughter of Sir Charles Appledore, 1888. Heir and only child, Lord Saltire... Well, well, this man is certainly one of the greatest subjects of the Crown!"

— "The Adventure of the Priory School"
The Return of Sherlock Holmes,
Sir Arthur Conan Doyle

"I WOULD warn your Grace, however, that the continued presence of Mr. James Wilder in your household can only lead to misfortune."

"I understand that, Mr. Holmes, and it is already settled that he shall leave me for ever and go to seek his fortune in Australia."

"In that case, your Grace, since you have yourself stated that any unhappiness in your married life was caused by his presence, I would suggest that you make such amends as you can to the Duchess, and that you try to resume those relations which have been so unhappily interrupted."

— "The Adventure of the Priory School"
The Return of Sherlock Holmes,
Sir Arthur Conan Doyle

JAMES WILDER's son, born off the shore of Andros Island, the Bahamas, was to become very famous.

— "A Case of a Case of Identity Recased, or,
The Grey Eyes Have It"
*Tarzan Alive: A Definitive Biography of
Lord Greystoke*,
Philip José Farmer

1.

A NIGHTMARE, PATRICIA thought. The trip from New York to London had been a nightmare of lightning streaks threatening the plane and vast buffetings and bellowings of thunder and airsickness. But the trip had been heaven compared to the real nightmare she was enduring now. The trip had seemed worth the trouble, because she could still envision the great house she would inherit. And she could imagine the great halls with their paintings of her ancestors, the dukes and duchesses, the earls and the countesses. She herself was going to be a baroness, if she decided to accept the legacy. But, before she ever got to Pemberley House, she was hurled into this nightmare. Stripped, hands and feet bound, eyes blindfolded, and the woman tonguing her.

This can't be, she thought, straining against the ropes and arching her body so that her spine hurt and her breasts threatened to lift off her body. This just can't be. Such things don't happen. Not in 1973. Not in the Midlands county of Derbyshire, England, a most civilized and pleasant place, at least, in the countryside, according to what she'd read. This could have happened to some of her ancestors. Something like this had happened to her many times great-grandmother, the one that was supposed to be haunting Pemberley House. But that had been in the 1570s. And this was now. Now!

Oh, God, she thought, and she tried to twist away. But her legs and arms were held far apart by ropes tied to something, stakes, probably. And that woman, who had been called Ernie, had taken off her own clothes and had eased down on her. Patricia had felt the smooth cool skin and the heaviness of the breasts being dragged across her face. Then they were on her mouth but lifted when Patricia tried to bite them. There had been a short coarse laugh, and then the breasts had dragged on down her stomach and on down.

She could scream and she probably would soon. But the fact that Ernie had not bothered to gag her meant that she was not worried about anyone hearing her. Neither was that man, whom Ernie had called Jack. And where was he now? Watching? Waiting until Ernie had done with her whatever she had in mind?

Patricia hoped she would not scream. It would do no good, obviously. And she did not want to give that swine the satisfaction of hearing her scream or begging for a mercy that she would never give even if she had it to give.

Perhaps she would not have to scream. So far, the two had been rough with her and had promised to cut her throat if she made any trouble. But Ernie had not hurt her. She had been unexpectedly gentle. But then she might be doing that to get her to relax and so hurt her even more when she did something painful. The sudden shock and the knowing that she was absolutely helpless, so helpless.

Tears ran down her cheeks, and she heard Ernie's rough, but undeniably female, voice say, "You're crying, baby. Is that because you feel so good? Do you like this?"

And Ernie's tongue moved up and down, slowly, and then her finger, coming in just below the tongue, began working back and forth. Patricia tried to move away; her flesh seemed to take on an independence and attempted to crawl away from her bones. But Ernie pressed her head down; her lips covered the hairiness and her nose pressed down the region just above the pubes. Patricia had felt somewhat sick at first, but as time passed and Ernie made no sudden moves and did nothing to give her pain, she relaxed a trifle. She did not want to relax; she wanted to die. Or so she told herself. But there was a tension coming through the numbness of shock and repulsion now, and adrenaline and fury began to course through her body.

And that, at least, was the best thing that had happened to her since she had gotten into the car at the Lambton railroad station, and that drunken Richard Deguy had started the big Rolls Royce with a scream of tires through the white-and-black and rainy night.

2.

ATRICIA CLARKE WILDMAN was 22 years old. She had been born in upstate New York and split her first seven years between there and Manhattan. Then her father had decided to retire, and he and his wife and their child had settled completely in upstate New York. Doctor Wildman's idea of retirement was to conduct the business of the isolated clinic which he had founded for the treatment and care of criminals and their rehabilitation. Though he had been a very well-known brain surgeon and biochemist, among other things, his hobby had been criminology. And so he had established the small *college*—as he called it—where men with records, seemingly hopeless criminals, were often turned out into society as first-rate citizens.

Patricia had not known until she was twenty that her own mother had been one of her father's patients and a graduate of the clinic-college. Who, looking at her beautiful sexy mother, would ever have thought that she had been one of the most wanted confidence women in the U.S.? At one time Patricia would have worried about her heritage, but she was old enough, and well educated enough, not to believe in the inheritance of a criminal temperament. Besides, if such could be gotten through transmission of genes, her father's traits would have overbalanced them. He was the most beautiful man she had ever seen, and he was also the most incorruptible and the most rigidly moral. He was, like a god, perfect.

But he must have been remarkably repressed, too, she had had to admit. He had not married until he was fifty. But he was certainly not shy of anything that made a man a man in bed. Patricia knew that, since she had once accidentally seen him with her mother, not in bed, but on a big Kodiak bear skin rug before the fireplace in their big cabin near the clinic. That had been when she was nine, and she had been very jealous of her mother since. Though she had to admit that she had been jealous long before that.

Nevertheless, she loved her mother, though, in her honest moments, she had to admit that she had loved her father more. Still, she had loved both very much, and so, when the news came of their death while in his private plane far above the Arctic Circle, she had collapsed. Several weeks passed before she was able, shakily and still numb, to leave the little hospital on the clinic grounds. Her savior had been Doctor Verner, a handsome young man recently hired by her father. He had stayed with her throughout her confinement, being always there whenever she needed him. It was true that his devotion wasn't entirely due to his dispassionate interest in anyone who happened to be his patient. At least, Patricia did not think it was. He had not been backwards about his desire for her, and it wasn't long before the desire had become a love. At least, he had said it was true love, and he had asked her to marry him. Unlike her father, he had no intention of waiting until he was middle-aged before he took a wife.

Patricia was very attracted to him. She could easily get aroused when he was near. He had black curly hair and a profile that would have been pretty if the nose hadn't been just a little too bold and the chin a little too prominent. Or could she say they were "a little too" when the slight roughnesses were what rescued him from looking a little faggy and made him so masculine?

In any event, there had been one night when he had managed to strip her down to her panties and was about to take them off when she had decided that she was letting him get too far too fast. She wasn't old fashioned, but there was such a thing as being too easy. Besides, and this was probably what saved her, handsome and undeniably virile as he was, he was not the man her father was.

That had shocked her, and she would be a long time getting over the shock at that thought. Was she so hung up on her father that she would never find a man good enough for her?

At that moment, Denis Verner had his clothes off and his mouth gently sucking on her nipple. She was starting to push his head away and to tell him that they had to stop. She did not find it easy to do so, since she felt on fire, and the pleasure of his mouth on her breast and his finger sliding back and forth under her panties was swiftly turning into a near undeniable ecstasy. And he had stopped the movement of his hand on her and peeled the panties down and then he had pulled away from her nipple and was on his knees above her and starting to lift her legs so he could remove the panties.

It was strange. She had not wanted him to stop, and yet she felt herself moving away from him. And she thought of her father on that rug. He had been on his knees also before letting himself down. The fireplace flames had flickered over him, on that dark-bronze straight hair and the bronzeish skin and the muscles like snakes under the skin and on that enormous dark member which belonged to her mother and only to her and which she, Patricia, could never have.

Denis Verner was not lacking, and besides, she knew enough to discount the size of men's genitals. It was, so she had been told, the performance, not the size, that mattered.

But it made no difference how big or how small he was at that moment. She was moving away from him, in spirit, though not in body, and her body might as well have been moving away from him, too. A thousand miles away. She had gotten up and dressed while he stared speechless at her. She had told him that she did not care to go any further. It did not repulse her, and she liked him very much. But she was not ready to take a man into her. No, she wasn't worried about getting pregnant or diseased; she was a doctor's daughter—though some of them were often ignorant—and she knew how to take care of herself, and she was sure that, since he was a doctor, he knew how to take care of himself.

But she just did not want to go to bed with him. Perhaps, she was more moral than she had thought.

She could not tell Verner about the image of her father, of course. She did not even like to admit that image to herself, but it often came regardless of her wishes.

Verner had muttered something about something. It ended in "…teaser," and she knew what he had said, but she did not get angry. Perhaps she was a teaser, and if she were she knew why. At least, she knew the secondary motive. Why she was in love with her father was something she could not answer. Not fully. Most little girls fell in love with their fathers, even when they were bald and fat. No girl she knew had ever had a father so tall, so giant-like, in fact, or so muscular or so handsome or so completely master of everything he did. But that wasn't good enough. Rather, his virtues were not enough to account for the fact that she still loved her father at the age of 22. Something, she told herself, had kept her from maturing. She was still a little girl inside her grown woman's body.

And then the terrible event had happened. First, word that her father had radioed that one of the motors of his plane was mal-functioning. Then, he was going to try to land on the rocky ground below. Then, silence. And after that, nothing. The search planes had the approximate location where the plane had gone down, but they could find no sign of it, not even a piece of wreckage. Later, parties on foot went out from various places where they had been set down by helicopters. But they had no luck. They could only conclude that the plane had fallen down into a narrow and deep valley and crashed through the ice over a stream. The ice had re-formed, and the plane was somewhere under the water and the ice. Even when the spring floods came, the plane might not be found. It could be covered with silt or torn apart on the rocks of rapids and the individual pieces whirled away and lost forever.

Patricia grieved. For days, she did not know where she was. Inside her 22-year-old woman's body, a little girl was trying to cry, but her bereavement was so great that it held down even the tears. She was frozen through and through.

It was Denis Verner who tried to unfreeze her and who tried first tender love and then sex. He seemed to think that his body held the key to unlocking the deep hurt in her body. And he was right, or, at least, half-right. He had asked her to marry him, and she, hardly realizing what she was saying, had said yes. They were married three days later in the city hall of the town near the clinic, and an hour later she was in bed with Denis. Or was she on that big Kodiak skin rug, and was that hot hard body pressing down on her and that hot hard thing moving back and forth inside her her father's?

It was only slowly that she did come out of the numbness, and when she did she had the grace to be ashamed of herself. It wasn't fair to Denis to let him make love to her while she was, in reality, being loved by her father. Thank God, she often thought later, she had not cried out, "Daddy! Daddy!" when she had felt the orgasm radiating out from her womb, like the circles that radiated outwards from a stone thrown in water. The circles that seemed to ripple her flesh with alternating heat and ice. She had what she thought was a peculiar reaction to sex; when the orgasm came, she became hot and cold in turn. Eventually, her legs and feet turned to ice, though the rest of her burned.

She remembered well that morning that she had decided that she would cast out the image of her father and replace it with Denis'. It wasn't fair to him to continue this love-making with her father's image while Denis was so much in love with her. She would, by some tremendous act of exorcism, eject her father. She would do this and thereby become healthy. Perhaps, then, she could weep, and the tears would wash out her father, and she could become a full-grown woman. The child would wash away with the tears.

And she could then grieve honestly for her mother, too. She felt guilt because she had not missed her mother, because she had thought only of the dead father. She had thought she had loved her mother. Her mother had always been kind and gentle and had usually been there whenever her daughter needed her. She had always made over Patricia, had always kissed and caressed her, played games with her, read to her. Why then, Patricia thought desperately, why then didn't she grieve for her mother? Why did she just think of her father?

Thinking of this, she had gotten out of bed and walked across the room to the full-length wall mirror. She was naked; her long dark-bronze hair was tumbled and messed up from Denis' hands. Her heavy but shapely breasts were red and bore toothmarks where Denis had failed to restrain himself. Her thighs bore faint bruises where he had gripped them, and her skin, reddish-bronze—like her father's, she thought—was shining with sweat and the wetness from his tongue where he had licked her. He had just left her; he was late for the clinic and so had dressed hastily, shaved with an electric razor, washed his face and hands, and run off. He had waved her a kiss as he went out; she had lifted an arm and waved languidly. She felt heavy, sated; this was the first time that she had been able to think of him as her young husband. She had seen her father's face flicker away and Denis' flicker in. She had not been able to hold his face before her; it kept pulsing in and out, alternating with her father's. But she was satisfied that she was making progress, and that some day she would see only Denis' face. And when he plunged again and again into her body, she would think of that "thing," as her father's...no, no, she meant, as Denis'. And it wasn't a thing, it was what Denis called it and what so many of her college girl friends had called it. But she found it hard to think of it in the four-letter terms her friends at school used so casually. She had had a somewhat sheltered life, in that her parents had been with her more than children of her age, and they had imposed a certain restraint on her. She had been given an unusual education; she had had many tutors who were world-famous in their specialties, and had undergone rigorous physical and mental training, two hours daily; she had gone with her parents on trips around the world, on expeditions to Africa and New Guinea and the Arctic. But her contacts with her contemporaries had been limited. She had known mostly adults. And it was this, strangely enough, that had kept her from fully growing up.

She thought of this as she looked at her long slim legs, her narrow waist, the curving bell-shaped hips and the thick curly dark-bronze pubic hair which Denis had said was the softest and the most delightful he had ever kissed. She looked at her breasts, which Denis had said were exactly right, large but not too large, firm yet soft, and with the biggest and pinkest nipples he had ever seen. It was a body to be proud of he had said, a body that should be immortalized in marble. Denis, of course, was exaggerating, but she liked to hear him talk about it.

Her face was a feminine variation of her father's. She had his light-brown eyes with the strange golden flecks that so caught people's attention. Her eyebrows were very thick but long and naturally arching and naturally black. Her eyelashes were also very long; she had never used artificial lashes.

Denis had not gotten such a bad deal, she was thinking. He loved her very much, and he was very proud of her, and she was going to see to it that he was not cheated. She would get rid of that sickness—admit it, it was a sickness—and expel her father from her mind—and her body—while she was in bed with Denis.

She stood there for a few moments, thinking of the love-making that had taken place fifteen minutes ago, and then she turned away. She put on her robe and started for the kitchen, and a knock sounded on the front door. She made sure her robe was buttoned and ran a comb quickly through her hair and then opened the door.

The man who stood there in a white laboratory jacket, his face twisted and white, was Robert Simmons, Denis' assistant. He stuttered for a few seconds before he managed to get the terrible news out.

Denis had been stabbed by a patient, stabbed with one of his own surgical tools. The criminal was mad, no doubt of that. He had no reason to kill Denis; Denis was going to operate on his brain to remove a tumor which had been found during a routine examination. But the patient had thought that Denis meant to cut out part of his brain and so reduce him to a robot. Even now, he was babbling of what Denis had intended to do to him after he had made him his mental slave. But Denis, Denis would never operate on the man or on any man. Nor would he be able to talk, as his killer was talking at this moment.

Nor would he ever make love to her, kiss her, and lovingly strip her and kiss her all over and make love with her.

Her parents had died two months ago. And now Denis, her lover, was dead.

3.

S HE HAD WANTED to die, too. But another man had come to her rescue. He was not young and handsome, as her dead Denis Verner had been, and he had never said anything about loving her. But Doctor Leonard Miller had known her since she was a baby, and he had seen her almost every day since she was seven. He was her father's partner, though he looked his age, while her father had always seemed twenty years younger than he actually was. Doctor Miller was 70, exactly the age of her father, but his hair was white, whereas her father's had kept its original dark-bronze color (though he may have been using a dye, of course). And her father did not have the wrinkles that Miller had (though he may have had some operations to take care of that). And her father's body was not fat or saggy or skinny, as other 70-year-old men were. He exercised without fail two hours every day and still had a body to command admiration whenever he went swimming or played handball.

(Why do I still keep comparing every man with Daddy? she had thought.)

Doctor Miller gave her sedatives and talked to her for long hours every day. He did not get her to feeling that life was worth living, but he did get her to quit thinking so strongly of taking cyanide. By that time, Doctor Miller was forced to leave the clinic, and Patricia was seeing another part of her life coming to an end. The clinic-college had run out of funds; the seemingly inexhaustible money had suddenly stopped. Moreover, a court order had temporarily suspended operations at the clinic while the murder of Doctor Verner was being investigated. It seemed that some of the patients had complained that they were being forced to endure certain scientific experiments; they felt their civil rights were being violated. This was not true, since every patient had been allowed to sign release papers only after the executives were sure that he understood exactly what he was signing.

By then, Patricia did not care what happened to the clinic. She walked around the high hills of the New York valley all day, thinking, trying to stop thinking, and came home tired every evening. She ate a little but not enough and began to look gaunt. Her breasts were not as large, she noticed, and the nipples had lost some of the pinkishness that Denis had gotten so poetic about. And her ribs were beginning to show.

Doctor Miller had tried to do something about this, though he had not been very subtle. He had introduced her to the young lawyer who was to defend the clinic. He had tried to throw Henry MacArthur into contact with her at every possible moment, and it was evident that he hoped that Henry would use the same methods to unfreeze her that Denis had used. Under somewhat different circumstances, MacArthur might have had a chance. He was certainly inclined to take Patricia to bed, and he was a beautiful young man, even if his chin was a little too long. He wore his hair long, and he sported a ruff of black hair on his chin and two enormous sideburns, and he wore ruffled shirts and very tight brightly striped pants. They were skin-tight and so rounded out hugely in the crotch. The first time he kissed Patricia, he pressed against her. He had her up against the wall of her living room, by the doorway, and he was reaching out with one hand to close the door. Evidently, he had changed his mind about leaving; he was hoping that she would not object, that she would allow him to close the door. The hardness against her told her that Henry was not wearing a codpiece, that it was all him under the white and red and black stripes of his pants.

For a moment, she almost let Henry have his way. Why not? She liked him, though she was far from loving him. And perhaps she might be able to forget for a few hours the tragedies that had come so closely one after the other. And if she were still a little girl inside herself, her body had its demands. She wanted the closeness of bare warm flesh and the feel of lips against hers and a tongue sliding into her mouth and a mouth on her nipples and lips sliding down her stomach and the tongue tracing along the border of her hair, and…She pushed him away and said, "No! Sorry, Henry! If it's going to be anyone now, it'd be you. But I don't want anyone at all. Not at this time."

She did not try to explain. What did she owe him? Nothing. He wasn't her father or Denis, and he would never be able to take their places, and if he stayed for the night it would be bad for both of them. She'd hurt him by her coldness—she knew she'd be cold, despite her need—and she didn't want to have to explain what was wrong with her.

That very next day, she got the letter from England. It stunned her, and yet it saved her life. Or, if not her life, her sanity. It opened a new world for her; it gave her something to do that she had never done before. And it would take her away from this place and its memories and ghosts.

There were some puzzling things about the letter, which was from the old and well-known (in England) firm of Marten, Petres, and Newell. Her father had mentioned that his father had been born in England and had left it when he was about 21 years old. He was born in the town of Lambton, Derbyshire county, had gone to Rugby, Eton, and King's College, Cambridge, and left shortly after graduation for Australia.

He had discovered enough gold there to finance a trip to the United States with his young wife, whom he may or may not have married in England before leaving it. Not that there was any doubt that James Wildman had formed a legal union with the French-Norwegian girl. Doctor Wildman had the documents to prove that. But she had died about a year after giving birth to the golden-eyed infant, and little Clarke had been raised by his father and the succession of tutors hired by his father to give his son the best of educations.

Her grandfather had died in 1931, and all she knew about him were the few facts her father had let drop and a photograph. This had been taken in the early 1900s and showed, in color, a handsome young man with dark red hair, a clean-shaven and intelligent face, and light blue eyes. His trousers were rather tight and bulged at the crotch. When Patricia had seen that photograph at the age of ten, she had, of course, noticed the bulge. And she had, of course, been unable to keep from picturing what was under the pants. The image of her father's great and rigid organ just before it entered her mother entered her mind. Entrance, she had thought while reading the letter from the English lawyer. My father entered my mother, and he entered my mind also. It was as if that enormous throbbing blood-filled "thing" sank into the vagina of my mind. But where it became soft and withdrew from my mother, it has always remained great and hard and thrusting, eternally thrusting, inside my brain. But it never explodes in orgasm, ejaculates, shrinks, and then slides out of the recesses of my memory. It stays there, forever erect.

She had tried to put that thought away with the photograph of her grandfather, James Clarke Wildman. She had then picked up the companion photograph of her grandmother. The girl was very pretty, and it was evident from her coloring who had supplied the bronze-red hair and the bronzeish skin and the golden eyes in the Wildman family. Poor unhappy creature, Patricia thought, putting that photograph away also. To die so soon after bearing your first child. She couldn't have been over twenty when they put her away forever in the Manhattan graveyard.

Patricia thought of this as she read the letter from England. Her grandfather, James Wildman, had not been just another young Englishman leaving the country to look for fame and fortune. He had been the son of the sixth Duke of Greystoke, first Marquess of Exminster, first Viscount Passmore, and a baronet.

The man with all these titles had been William Cecil Fitzwilliam Clayton, a very prominent statesman of the late Victorian and of the early Edwardian periods. According to Burke's *Peerage*, "His lordship [the sixth Duke] purchased Pemberley House from his cousin, Sir Gawain Darcy [Bt.], who had purchased it from Fitzwilliam Bennet Darcy when that gentleman suffered great financial reverses." His son was to inherit all these titles and the great estate of Pemberley House and Pemberley Woods and many other lands, in addition to valuable mining properties and industries.

Unfortunately for James Wildman, he was not the son who would inherit all this. He was the oldest son of the duke, but he was also the illegitimate son. Sometimes bastards, or natural sons, as they were called in Burke's *Peerage*, inherited the title and the property. But it was not to be in this case. Everything went to the younger, but legitimate, son. And so James Wildman, although raised by the duke after his mother died, and educated by the duke, and even given a job as the duke's private secretary for a while, had left England. The lawyer, Mr. Newell, hinted that James Wildman had left under rather peculiar circumstances. It was obvious that if Patricia wanted to know the details, she would have to ask Mr. Newell in the privacy of his office when—or if—she got to London.

Patricia did not remember her father ever saying anything about his father's early life except for the few educational statistics. Perhaps he had not known about them. There was nothing about them in the papers that she had gone through.

She read on. The younger son had inherited the titles and the properties when the sixth duke died in 1909. He had died several months ago, in 1972, along with his wife Jane, under mysterious circumstances, at the age of eighty-one.[1] But his mother still lived, Mr. Newell stated. She was amazingly healthy and bright for a woman of 103 years; she might live for another decade. After all, Mr. Newell said, the greatest authenticated age a human being had reached was 113 years and 124 days. The Canadian Pierre Joubert had lived that long, from 1701 to 1814. An American had lived 112 years and two others had lived 111 years, and Margaret Ann Neve of the Channel Islands had lived 110 years and 321 days. He cited others who had attained the ages of 109 and 108, but Patricia skimmed through these to what interested her the most.

The dowager duchess was still alive, but she was in line for a reasonable pension alone, though this included quarters for the rest of her life in Pemberley House. If no one had been left in the direct line of descent, then she would have inherited much of the property.

Her grandchildren would inherit nothing because they were adopted. Rather, they were the children of her adopted son, who was dead, Mr. Newell corrected himself. If Patricia were to die soon, or turn the inheritance down, then the grandchildren of the dowager duchess would inherit. These, Mr. Newell said, were twins, Richard and Carla Deguy. They were living in Pemberley House now, and Miss Wildman would undoubtedly meet them if she came to England. For her convenience, he had enclosed photographs of them, along with those of others.

The glossy showed two young people, arm in arm, facing the camera and smiling. They certainly looked like twins, she thought, and they were certainly handsome. Richard reminded her of Richard Greene, the English movie star who had also played Robin Hood in the TV series. She had had a crush on him when she was a child, though he took second place in her affections to her father, of course.

Carla looked like a feminine version of Richard Greene, a very sexy version. She was wearing a tight blouse and shorts—perhaps she had been playing tennis or cricket—or did the women in England play cricket?—and her breasts filled the cloth and seemed to be trying to get out. They had half-succeeded; the blouse was cut very low. In fact, now that Patricia examined the picture, she was not sure that Carla was wearing a bra under the sheer white material. It certainly did not look like it, and the nipples were rather dark under the cloth. Yes, she wasn't wearing a bra. Which meant that the girl had a magnificent pair of breasts, because there was no sag at all.

Richard Deguy, her brother, was also wearing tight shorts, and there, as she knew it would be, was a prominent bulge. Were all the men she knew heavily endowed or was it just that her memory of her father was influencing her mentally, and so she was seeing things that did not exist? Well, she thought, and she laughed mentally for the first time in a long time, she couldn't be seeing things that did not exist, because all those men must have genitals. But she could be exaggerating what she thought.

On the other hand, if Richard Deguy were as well equipped as his sister, only in a different place of course, then he did indeed bulge in his tight shorts.

She sighed and thought, You're living in the midst of more than one kind of shadow, my friend.

She put down the photograph and looked at the others. One was of a handsome old woman of about seventy, identified as the Duchess of Greystoke. Rather, the ex-duchess now. She had dark and thick eyebrows and a sharp curving nose and thin lips. The description did not make her sound beautiful, but she must have been very attractive, nevertheless, when she was younger. Mr. Newell stated that this was the last photograph of her of which he knew. He had, however, seen her ten years ago, when she was only 93 (only? Patricia thought), and she had aged somewhat since then, he understood. But she still did not look her age.

Mr. Newell continued with some facts about the estate and then got down to the essentials. If Miss Wildman (evidently he had not learned that she was married—had been married) were to come to England, she would be given all particulars. For the time being, she should be interested to know that she was the only heir, or heiress, in the direct line of descent. She would not inherit any of the titles except that of the Baroness of Lambton. The other titles, according to the limitations of the patents, would become extinct. Only male heirs of the body, as Mr. Newell put it, could succeed to the other titles, and none of these existed. Therefore, Miss Wildman was in line to be the next Baroness of Lambton; the rank derived from a feudal barony associated with the Pemberley estate itself, although some previous holders had refused the title.

However, Mr. Newell continued, there was precedent for special grants being approved to preclude the extinction of a peerage—or rather, to cause its revival by bestowing upon someone else with new letters patent. If Miss Wildman wished, Mr. Newell would begin proceedings to apply for the special grant. In the meantime, pursuant to the barony, she was entitled to be addressed as Baroness Wildman or Lady Wildman. If the special grant was made, then she would be the Duchess of Greystoke.

There had been many properties and businesses in the family when the sixth duke died, Mr. Newell said. Unfortunately, the seventh duke, William Cecil Arthur Clayton, had not paid attention to business as he should. He and his late wife Jane also, Mr. Newell hinted, had certain habits which had been expensive, to say the least. As a result of these, and also of death duties and the heavy taxation which had plagued England for more years than Mr. Newell cared to think about, the Lancashire, Cumberland, and Wales properties were things of the past. The estate in Kenya had been disposed of separately. But she would, if she decided to accept the inheritance, have Pemberley House and Pemberley Woods as hers and a considerable amount of stock in railways and several London and Manchester banks.

Patricia was numbed after reading the letter. But the next day she felt the numbness being peeled off by an excitement that could not be repressed. Here was a chance to get away from the clinic, which depressed her so with its many sad memories. And here was a chance to enter a brand new world, one which might make her forget, might help heal her grief. And though she had always laughed at titles, as any American was supposed to do, yet, like most Americans, she had a certain respect for the ancient British titles beneath the seeming scorn.

What would it be like to be addressed as Baroness? Baroness Wildman? Did this title give her the right to sit in the House of Lords? No, it did not, she quickly found out in the *Encyclopaedia Britannica*. The barony was not a hereditary peerage. Even if she instructed Mr. Newell to pursue the special grant, and she became the Duchess of Greystoke, she'd not be entitled to sit in the House of Lords. Not unless she became a British citizen.

Well, she thought, she would worry about that in the future. For the time being, she must get a letter off to Mr. Newell, tell him of her arrival time (which meant she must check out airline flights first), get a wardrobe together, write some letters to a few of her college friends, and settle business affairs with Doctor Miller and the board of directors of the clinic. They could do with it what they wanted. She was through with it, even if the English venture turned out sour. She wanted nothing more to do with the place that had, in a sense, murdered her husband and had taken so much of her father's time away from her.

A week later, she was on her way in a huge double-decker jet, and eleven days later she was in Derbyshire. But she had never, even in her most far-out fantasies, envisioned anything such as this as the journey's end. Here she was, stripped, tied down, spread-eagled, and being licked all over by the lesbian, Ernie, and being penetrated in every aperture of her body by that long insistent tongue.

4.

$\mathcal{P}$ATRICIA HAD STAYED in London with a friend who lived in Mayfair. Roberta Macelhiney had married an Englishman she had met at Berkeley, and she had once invited Patricia to stay with her if she ever came to London. Patricia stopped off for a few days with her while she had several conferences with old Mr. Newell, who looked as if he were a contemporary of the dowager duchess, shopped, did the tourist bit around London, and reminisced with Roberta.

She talked on the phone once with Richard Deguy, who apologized for not coming to London to pick her up. But his grandmother had had a setback, he said, and neither he nor his sister thought it wise to leave her until she got better. He would have sent Austin, the chauffeur, down for her, but Austin had recently lamed his leg and would not be driving for a week, if then.

Richard's voice was a rich baritone, very masculine and masterful, and he sounded sincerely sorry.

Patricia said that it wasn't necessary to send anyone all the way down from Pemberley. She would take the railway from the Charing Cross station (she thought that was right but would look it up in the Bradshaw). And she would take a taxi from the Castle Hill station east of Lambton out to Pemberley House.

"Not at all, my dear," Richard Deguy said. "I'll be waiting at Castle Hill for you and will drive you in myself."

Roberta had lifted the phone in the downstairs hall at that moment, whether by accident or because of curiosity. Probably the latter, since Roberta was nosey. She had said, "Oh, excuse me!" and hung up. Later, she said to Patricia, "That man's voice sends shivers all through me! He's got testicles in his voice chords!"

Patricia laughed, but she was beginning to find Roberta's vulgarity rather wearing. She had forgotten that part of her, or, rather, had allowed time to soften it in her memory. Still, she was sorry to say goodbye to her. She represented the last link with the old world; from now on she would be in a very strange world. How strange she had no way of guessing, of course.

After she exited the taxi at Charing Cross station, Patricia had been almost flattened by a car that came around the corner as she was crossing the street. She escaped only by throwing herself between two parked cars. The offending car squealed off as if the driver had not seen her. She was unscathed but somewhat shaken up and disheveled with small bruises and cuts as a result of a hard landing on the asphalt between the parked cars.

Getting her legs under her, she tugged her miniskirt to cover a small snag in the upper left thigh of her stocking, got her breasts pushed back into the blouse which had popped the top buttons, and grabbed her luggage. She set off across the street again for the station and the Lambton train, the clacking of the heels on her black leather boots marking her determined stride.

The worst thunderstorm in years, according to the conductor, struck the southern boundary of Derbyshire just as the train crossed it. The lightning opened up the night as if it were trying to rip the lid off of hell itself. Barrages of thunder crossed the black sky, and the rain was so solid that it was easy to imagine that she was at the bottom of a disturbed river. Wind buffeted the cars, making them sway, and whenever the lightning permitted, she could see the trees bending down before the fury of the air.

Patricia sat in a compartment with an old man and his wife and two middle-aged men. The tall thin man with an aquiline face

and keen grey eyes smoked a pipe with no objections from the
tall green-eyed Chinese-looking man who sat by him. It was not,
however, until the train stopped at Matlock that Patricia understood why the two sat so closely together nor why the Chinese,
though he often wrinkled his aristocratic non-Chinese nose at the
powerful scent of the shag tobacco, did not get up and move. The
tall grey-eyed man rose, and with him, willy-nilly, came the tall
Chinese. They were handcuffed together.

Before leaving, the Chinese man turned to Patricia, his green
eyes blazing in the dim light of the compartment, and said to her,
"I knew your parents well, Miss Wildman. They were relentless,
although honorable, enemies of mine. Or at least your father was
honorable. You have my condolences." The other man tugged his
companion along, but not before piercing Patricia with his grey
eyes, as if he knew her—or her parents—as well.

Patricia never saw them again, but she often remembered
them. They were a bad omen, she would think later, an indication
of the strange things that were to come. From that time on, she
had entered, without a passport, a strange country, a weird and
nightmare land.

The two men left, and the old man and his old wife discussed
the policeman and his prisoner in soft tones. The old man had
been switching his attention from the peculiar couple to Patricia's
long legs and back to the couple. Now he devoted all of his attention her legs. Patricia tried to catch his eyes to stare him down, but
the old man, who looked like a retired vicar, refused to raise his
eyes. She crossed her legs and lowered her eyes to the magazine
propped on her leg and quit trying to embarrass him. If the old
man got a charge out of feeling her legs with his eyes, and God
knew what else he was doing in his imagination, why, let him. He
couldn't be hurting her, and he might be doing himself some good.
Perhaps, if he became aroused enough, he might even take his wife
to bed.

She read several articles in the magazine and decided that
it was almost impossible to get away from sex. The first article
told of the new variation of the Hump-the-Hostess game current

in certain circles in Westchester, New York, and Beverly Hills, California. The second described the circumcision ceremony for twelve year old girls in a Central African tribe. Apparently, the local witch doctor bit the clitorises out with his filed teeth. Patricia had read much, and she had never heard of this method of female circumcision. Most tribes, such as the Wantso, prohibited men from being present at female circumcision ceremonies. Patricia looked at the cover of the magazine, which showed a distraught woman holding a baby that seemed to be half-snake. MY HUSBAND'S PET PYTHON MADE LOVE TO ME was spread in big black letters over the gaudy sheet.

She put the magazine, face down, on the seat and leaned back and closed her eyes. The car swayed with the wind's hammering. The thunder boomed. The rain was striking the windows by her.

And I suppose, she thought, that old man is having an emotional storm inside himself while he's looking at my legs and at that part of my derriere which isn't covered by my miniskirt. You can't get away from storms. Even if you could get away from Nature's and from your own, you can't get away from other people's. Not unless you go to a desert island, and there aren't any more desert islands. There are people everywhere, and with them there are storms.

She must have gotten away, though, because she suddenly sat up and knew that she had been sleeping. The train was slowing, and the old couple was getting ready to leave the compartment.

Patricia got her two suitcases down from the racks and carried them out. They were large and heavy, but she was a big girl and in excellent condition. She might have been rendered numb by recent events, she thought, but she was not as helpless as people seemed to think. She'd be coming out of her emotional deep freeze soon, especially now that she was in a new and exciting world. That old man didn't know, when he was looking at her legs, that they belonged to a future baroness.

When she got off the coach at Castle Hill, she stepped into a wind that tore at her and a downpour that came close to being a flash flood. The lights from the station house were feeble, and so she could not get a clear view of the face of the young man who helped her off the coach and took her bags. The collar of his coat was turned up, and the brim of his hat was pulled down. But she recognized the deep rich baritone when he spoke to her. And when they got inside the station, he removed his hat, and she could see that he was Richard Deguy. He looked a little older than he had in the photograph and more than somewhat jaded. He breathed the fumes of bourbon at her, but at least they were from a good bourbon.

"Beastly weather," he said, grinning, "though not fit for beasts. But, therefore, good enough for me. Or does that make any sense? Never mind, this is no night for making sense."

She held out her hand and said, "I'm pleased to meet you, Mr. Deguy. And it was nice of you to come out in this weather and drive me to Pemberley."

"We're not all that formal in merry new England," he said, laughing. "Call me Richard, coz, and I'll call you Patricia, or is it Pat? We are related, you know, even if my relationship comes only through adoption. Otherwise...well, no use talking about that."

Richard's twin sister, Carla, had stayed at the estate with the dowager duchess. "She keeps on hanging on. Still sharp at 103.[2] After all, the family motto is *Ung Viveray*. Means one will survive or one will live. Anyway, come along. She wants to see you as soon as we get there."

He picked up the bags and started walking toward the back of the station. The only other people in the little building were the station master and a young woman sitting on a bare wooden bench. She looked pretty, though in a cheap way, and Patricia was surprised when Richard stopped in front of her and let the bags down. The woman rose to her feet, and, though she had a coat buttoned around her, she was evidently pregnant. About five months along, Patricia thought.

"Rosamond Aylward," Richard said. "Miss Wildman, from the States."

"Mrs. Verner," Patricia said. "You forgot I told you over the phone that..."

"Oh, yes," Richard said. "You did say you were recently widowed. Terribly sorry about that. Well, come along. I hope you don't mind our going a little bit out of the way, Patricia. I must run Rosie here up to her father's tavern. It's only a few miles north of Pemberley, and she'd have to take a taxi, and it's beastly difficult to get a taxi this time of night and in such hellish weather."

"No, of course I don't mind," Patricia said.

The woman had only nodded when she had been introduced to Patricia, and, from the sullen expression, she was not going to talk at all. Her eyes looked red, as if she had been crying, though the beer fumes she was expelling indicated that the redness might have come from another cause. Patricia wondered what had been going on between these two. Evidently, they had been waiting for her for some time, though not in the station. Probably in the little tavern across from the station, she thought. Whatever they had been talking about, it had angered her.

They ran from under the shelter of the overhang to a large grey car, a Rolls, Patricia thought. Richard opened the back door and motioned for Patricia to get in. She climbed in, expecting the Aylward girl to follow her. But Richard Deguy slammed the back door and opened the left front for Aylward. She drew back, almost as if she were thinking about refusing to get in, but he slapped her on the rear and shouted something which Patricia couldn't hear because of thunder. Rosamond got in and shut the door herself, because he had run around to the right side.

"The bags," Patricia said. "You forgot the bags."

"What?" Richard said, and he turned around to look at her. "Oh, yes, the bags! Well, I'll be damned!"

He got out again and trudged around the car, opened the trunk, put the bags in, slammed the trunk lid, and got back into the car. Patricia did not say anything, but she wondered if he was fit to drive. Perhaps he had been drinking even more than she thought. Still, his speech wasn't slurred. He might just be thinking about the girl.

The Rolls started, and they drove out onto a road on which were few cars and few lights from houses. Richard drove faster than she cared for in this driving rain, but she said nothing. He asked her a few questions about her life in America and how she liked London.

"It's crazy, I've been all over the world with my parents, but never spent any length of time in England, although I grew up on stories of many famous and infamous ancestors. I've wondered often why we didn't spend more time here. To be honest, though, everything has been off since I arrived. I was almost hit by a car in the streets of London, a dirty old vicar on the train kept undressing me with his eyes, and two other strange men on the train seemed to know me—and my late parents." Patricia sank back further into the soft leather of the back seat. "Right now all I want is a hot bath and bed."

"Gods, what a beastly night you've had. Well, I'm sure that bath and bed will be all arranged when we arrive at Pemberley House," murmured Richard, and then quit trying to make conversation with her.

Rosie had been sitting as far away from Richard as possible, but when he said something in a low tone to her, she moved closer. He continued to talk in a voice too low for Patricia to catch his words. His tone was evident, however; he was trying to make up with her whatever needed making up.

Patricia was disgusted. If he wanted to carry on with this girl, who was not of his class and who was probably carrying his child, that was his business. But he was certainly not showing good manners by ignoring his guest and conducting a love affair in front of her.

She settled back and closed her eyes. He hoped that he wouldn't get so wrapped up with the girl that he would neglect his driving. The visibility was very poor, and the roads must be slick. And the way the wind was buffeting the car, it could be pushed a little out of its lane just at the wrong moment. There were not many cars on the highway, but one could come along at a fatal time. She was glad they were driving in a big heavy car, which resisted the wind more than, say, an English Ford or Hillman.

Suddenly, Patricia opened her eyes, and she thought, Oh, no!

Rosamond was no longer visible. From the front seat was a sucking noise, and Richard was groaning, though in a very low voice.

Patricia closed her eyes again but clenched her hands. He had not only talked her out of her anger, but he had talked her into demonstrating that she was truly reconciled. Or perhaps it was her idea. In either case, both must be more drunk than she had suspected. Or else young English people were even more uninhibited than she read they were.

Patricia felt sick, although she had no moral reasons for objecting to fellatio. She had been rather isolated from girls and boys of her own age when a child, but she had always been allowed to read anything she wished. And she had had some of the greatest anthropologists and psychologists in the world as her tutors during the summer. Her father had been willing to pay the high sums they demanded so she could have the very best education. (But she wondered now why, if he were so intelligent, and if the psychologists were so perceptive, they had not made sure that she had more playmates of her age.)

She had read about strange sexual customs when in eighth grade. In fact, she had books in her library which contained many photographs of couples, and sometimes groups, in every conceivable sexual position. These had disturbed her somewhat, though she would not admit that they did so to her teachers. And so, when she had watched her mother performing fellatio on her father, she had not been disgusted by the act itself, but she had been sick with envy. Her beautiful mother, dead now, and so young, younger than her father had been when he had finally married, had possessed her father in every way Patricia had ached to and couldn't.

In the back seat of the Rolls, thinking of her father, Patricia groaned and moved her fingers back and forth against the slick wetness under her skirt, and slipped a couple fingers in and out, her eyes still clamped shut.

Then she gasped again, or was it Richard, and she saw the back of Rosamond's head appear again. The big car pulled up next to a two-story building, and Patricia could barely make out the sign Fighting Cock lit by dim yellow lamps through the driving rain.

Fighting cock indeed, thought Patricia. I'm fighting for my father's, which is stupid. Even if he was alive, I couldn't have it.

Richard and Rosamond got out and he walked her just inside the door, and Patricia cleaned herself up. Then he was back behind the wheel, water pouring off his raincoat, and they were driving again.

"Sorry about that, coz," he said, "not far now, we'll be there shortly."

Patricia made some noise in response, and shook her head. Was he sorry for the side trip or his own behavior?

She decided she didn't care.

She stared out the car window at the passing oaks of the Pemberley Woods, down a deserted road, the headlights penetrating the dark tunnel of trees and overhanging branches. Down the dark tunnel into Wonderland, Patricia thought, with me cast as Alice and Richard as the Mad Hatter.

They descended even farther into the pitch darkness, and Richard took another stab at conversation. "I guess you'll be the Baroness, eh?"

"I suppose," Patricia said. "That's what Mr. Newell said. I really haven't studied the intricacies of British titles."

"Well, you'll learn, you have enough nobility in your bloodline, I guess. For instance, your ancestor, Bess. She wasn't nobility, but she did start the line."

"Bess?"

"Of course, coz, Bess d'Arcy." Richard turned slightly to look back at Patricia and the Rolls slid a little on the slick roadway.

"Watch the road!" Patricia said.

Richard turned back around. "Nothing to it, been down this stretch a thousand times." He chuckled. "So you never heard of your illustrious ancestress, Bess d'Arcy? Married four times, it's said, the last to William d'Arcy, the Baron of Lambton. Killed her in a murderous rage, the story goes, the day old Bess gave birth to their daughter, Jane. Except maybe she wasn't William's daughter, if you know what I mean."

Although she couldn't see him, Patricia could imagine him winking at her. Lecher. "What does this have to do with anything?"

"The curse, Pat, the curse. Didn't you know?"

"What curse? You're not making any sense. And it's Patricia. Would you *please* watch the road?"

"Sure, coz, of course, no need to get cross." He grinned. "Besides, didn't I say this wasn't the night for making sense? Making love, maybe." A whiff of the bourbon came drifting back at her.

"Making love, maybe, but you've had plenty of that already, and plenty to drink too. Just get us there in one piece, please, it's been a hell of a day already."

"Of course, Patricia. But I'll finish telling you about the Pemberley Curse."

Lightning flashed and thunder shook the car. Crooked branches reached for the Rolls but the vehicle raced by, just out of grasp.

Richard continued. "Perfect night for it. Anyway, William had killed Bess's lover, a sea captain named Fermier, and nine months later he killed Bess herself. Jane d'Arcy grew up right here at Pemberley House, a poor unhappy creature. On the night of her twenty-second birthday, back in 1592, happiness was finally in sight as she celebrated her engagement—and escape from her lunatic father, by the way—when lo and behold a relative of Fermier's, a self-styled sorcerer named Baron de Musard, shows up and curses the old man." Richard chuckled again as another round of lightning struck nearby. "All a bunch of rot, but fun rot at that."

"If you think that story is funny," Patricia said, "I'd hate to hear you tell a sad tale."

"But Patricia, it gets better. You see, old William d'Arcy in his madness—or maybe in his cups—killed his daughter Jane that night, the night of her birthday, mistaking her for the ghost of Bess, and now the curse is passed from generation to generation.

"A few months later, de Musard was found in his château in France, with every bone in his body shattered. By all accounts, the sorcerer was beaten to death by a chap called Sir John Gribardsun—that's a mouthful!—some distant relative of Jane's fiancé.

"Interesting, but what's the curse?"

"Oh, that. Gloomy dead Bess appears on the anniversary of her murder, but only to family members in her direct line of descent, and only in Pemberley House itself. The Baroness' ghost appears at 12 o'clock midnight for three nights in a row: the night before, the night of, and the night after the anniversary."

"Now you are telling ghost tales," Patricia said. "How could the curse be passed to subsequent generations if William d'Arcy killed his own daughter, before she had children?"

"Silly girl, the whole family was cursed. It was passed to the children of Jane's older brother, Christopher d'Arcy, and their descendants. You can look it all up in Burke's *Peerage* tomorrow, we have a copy in the library. You really should familiarize yourself with your own ancestry." He paused and then added, "I have."

"Are you trying to say I'm a direct descendent, that I'm subject to this so-called curse?" Patricia asked.

"Come now, Patricia, you shouldn't worry about it, yes, you're in the direct line, but it's just a beastly legend. It's just on all our minds because the anniversary is in two nights." He laughed.

"Anyway, there're more serious matters to worry over. There are some poachers about, and the gamekeeper, Parker—Parker, get it?" Richard laughed at his own joke.

It was a bad habit, Patricia thought. And the deep baritone of his voice wasn't so attractive any more.

"Parker is out looking for them now. In fact, as I told you earlier, the chauffer, Austin, is down with a lame leg. Two poachers came after him and he was hurt getting away. The police have been to the estate but have done nothing."

They went around a bend in the road, and lightning struck again. Ahead of them on the road, two masked people were mounted on motorcycles, with guns.

"Shit!" Richard sent the car off the road, avoiding the two people, and gunshots exploded, although none hit the Rolls. Richard skidded the car around, turned, and came back the opposite way.

"What the hell are you doing," yelled Patricia. "Keep going, you idiot."

Richard's car hit one cycle, but the rider was only slightly hurt. As the Rolls sped by in the direction opposite it had come, the masked cyclists shot out the tires. The car spun out on the rain-slicked surface and hit a tree hard. Patricia's head collided against the side window and she was knocked out.

Patricia woke up briefly as the two cyclists dragged her out of the car. Richard was nowhere to be seen. Perhaps he had fled into the woods. One of the cyclists hefted her over a shoulder in a fireman's carry and they headed up a hill. Half-blinded by the sheets of rain, Patricia made out a dim shape, tall and narrow, jutting out of the top of the hill like a dark, swollen phallus. She vaguely remembered that this must be the ruined structure behind Pemberley House, Mary's Tower, and then passed out again.

| 5.

Now here she was, arms and legs tied to ropes staked in the ground, being tongued by her captor, the woman Ernie. She was blindfolded so that she couldn't identify Ernie.

Patricia had come to again in the Tower, already tied and staked down and blindfolded, but had feigned unconsciousness. There were two who had snatched her, as far as she could tell.

The man, whom Ernie called Jack, said, "I can't find him, he ran off into the woods." He had a thick Cockney accent.

"It wasn't him, you stupid fuck, he wasn't driving. Don't you know anything?" Ernie's voice was coarse, harsh, and yet there was a hint of refinement in it somewhere. Or at least there had used to be.

"Well, what about this bird, what's she going to say?" Jack sounded worried.

"Maybe nothing," Ernie said, and Patricia twitched involuntarily.

"Hey, hey, what's this, is the little birdie awake?" Jack tweaked one of Patricia's bronze-colored hairs, and she started.

"Who are you, sweetie?" Ernie asked. "Tell the truth now, and we won't hurt you."

Patricia had told them, and they went through her papers and passport.

"That's it, we shouldn't have nabbed this one."

"What'll we do now, Ernie," Jack whined. "We don't know how long she's been awake. She may've heard our names."

"Well if she didn't before, she did just now, *Jack Hare*. God, you're a stupid fuck." Ernie turned and spoke to Patricia, caressing her cheek. "You won't tell, will you dearie?"

Patricia said no, of course not. "Please, just let me go."

"Promise not to talk, not a word, and we'll let you go. But if you talk we'll slit your throat. Right, *Jack?*"

"Yeah," came Jack's voice. "But hey, Ern— Well, it's been a while and look at her, she's sex on legs."

Ernie considered this, then said, "All right, we'll jump her, but make it fast."

They had stripped Patricia down quickly, pulling down her skirt, tearing off her blouse and bra, and ripping open her nylons at the crotch.

"Look at that jack and danny," breathed Jack Hare, but Ernie was already elsewhere, having taken off her own top and dangling her breasts above Patricia's mouth, and then planting her own mouth on Patricia's large pink nipples, sucking and nipping at them.

Jack made to let himself down on Patricia, but Ernie inched her way down and pushed him away. "Back off, you'll get your turn," she growled and then she went down between Patricia's legs, and ran her tongue back and forth.

Patricia responded, to her horror, although tears streaked her cheeks. "You're crying, baby. Is that because you feel so good? Do you like this?" Ernie asked her.

Patricia hated her helplessness. She hated the chafing of the ropes on her wrists, the lack of leverage that kept her pinned to the ground. She hated every minute of the day that had led her to this awful moment.

But most of all, she hated the woman called Ernie.

And as fear and rage and took over, fueled by the adrenal gland releasing its flight-or-flight hormone into Patricia's bloodstream, thews and sinews rippled under bronzed skin and tightened.

Ropes snapped and the hastily hammered in stakes, which had held her spread-eagled, ripped out of the ground.

Before the two abductors knew what happened or could react by pulling their guns, Patricia stood before them, blindfold torn off, one wooden stake in each hand. Her blouse was in tatters, one sleeve still attached at the wrist. Her stockings hung in shreds on her long, bronze legs and over the black leather boots. And then one foot was in the air and connected under Jack Hare's chin and sent him reeling. He collapsed in a corner, spitting out blood and teeth.

Patricia advanced on Ernie and pounded on the woman with the wooden stakes. The stakes had restrained Patricia, been a part of her helplessness, and now she'd use them against her erstwhile assailant. She thrashed Ernie about the head and torso, and stopped only long enough to give Jack an occasional whack to keep him in check. Finally, the two gathered their wits, and Ernie her discarded clothing, and they fled in disarray.

Patricia was too exhausted to follow.

But she was clearly her father's daughter.

| 6.

T HE ROOM IN which Patricia had been held had bare
stone walls and a dirt floor. There were no windows
and a couple torches stuck in cast iron wall sconces
provided minimal light. The cell was probably underground. There
was a wooden door in one wall. Ernie and Jack, in their haste, had
left the door wide open. If they had been thinking, they would
have slammed the door and locked Patricia in, then regrouped
and decided what to do with her. The thought worried her and she
checked her impulse to barrel through the exit and into a potential
ambush, and instead opted to silently approach the open doorway,
dart her head into the corridor, and check for the two goons,
although she hadn't heard them return.

No, they hadn't been thinking, they were gone, or at least they
didn't lie in wait for her right outside the cell. Still, they could be
somewhere in the Tower, and Patricia thought she had better get
out fast.

She ducked back in the cell, grabbed her miniskirt and belt
and pulled them back on, and arranged her torn blouse to cover up
her naked breasts as best she could.

Then Patricia exited the room, holding the wooden stakes
at the ready, and entered the stone passageway. It was also lit

by torches in sconces, but only two, which showed the way to a winding staircase. She began the climb and after one circuit all was pitch black. She stopped when she thought she heard what sounded like pebbles bouncing and skittering across stone, but all she could hear now was the pounding rain and occasional rumble of distant thunder. This was a good sign and meant she was close to the surface and presumably the way out of the Tower. The distance of the thunder was also a good sign. The storm was moving off.

Patricia staggered out into the rain. There was still no sign of Ernie and Jack. She wandered around Mary's Tower a bit before she finally found a pathway which led downward from the top of the hill upon which the Tower stood. She continued and walked along a while until the path intersected with a wide, paved road, and instinctively turned right onto the road.

The rain, although now constant and absent the driving winds, had soaked her through and she was shivering. She felt like her distant ancestor Jane Bennet, sent by an uncaring and selfish mother to Netherfield in a rainstorm on horseback rather than enclosed carriage. Perhaps she'd get pneumonia like Jane had and almost perish. That would show her. She'd get back at her mother for being the object of her father's love in a way that she, Patricia, could never be. For being so beautiful. For dying and leaving her alone, to be attacked and assaulted like this.

Then Patricia recognized she was being silly and unfair. Her mother, Adélaïde, had loved her terribly and would have done anything to protect her. Patricia realized she missed her now, more than she ever had, and salty tears mingled with the rain. She was dizzy and exhausted and disoriented, and then the wrecked car was in front of her, and Richard was there and he bundled her into the Rolls, out of the rain.

"Thank God you're all right. I looked everywhere, but this damned storm made it impossible. Hang tight here. I'll lock the door and go get help."

"They held me prisoner," Patricia mumbled. "They might come back…"

"Whoever they were, coz, there shouldn't be any more trouble. They'll fear the police and just be on their way. Look, their cycles are gone, too. Stay here and I'll be back in a jiffy."

Richard locked the door and set off on foot.

Patricia must have dozed from fatigue because the next thing she remembered the police arrived and took Patricia and Richard to the Pemberley estate.

Doctor Augustus Moran, the personal physician who lived in the house and attended to the duchess, made an examination and gave Patricia a sedative after the police questioned her.

She saw and heard a man talking to police about the trouble they'd had with poachers, and she realized this must be Parker, the gamekeeper. Patricia reported that one of the poachers was a woman called Ernie and the other was a man called Jack; the police seemed concerned about this.

Then the trials of the day—from almost being killed by the speeding car in London, to Richard's unseemly behavior on the drive from the Lambton rail station, to the car wreck and kidnapping and assault, the fight, and the escape through the rainstorm—combined with the sedative to put Patricia into a deep, deep slumber.

| 7.

ATRICIA AWOKE THE next day to sunshine streaming in her room. She was in bed, a large antique wooden affair with four posts carved in various shapes that looked like gargoyles and nymphs and trolls. She was in her nightdress. She didn't remember changing out of her ruined clothing and hoped, or at least assumed, there were maids or whatever they were called in England—like Bertie Wooster's Gentleman's Gentleman, Jeeves, except for women, but the term escaped her—who had helped her undress and change and get into bed. The thought of more strangers groping and touching her was disconcerting—she didn't want to be touched—but presumably such a servant could be expected to be professional about it.

The curtains at the tall French windows had been drawn and daylight poured in. She sat up in bed and looked around the room. It was Elizabethan, with rough carved wooden chests, drawers, and settees. Tapestries and paintings hung on the walls. A large gilt-edged mirror, taller and wider than Patricia, was mounted on the wall opposite her bed. The room had two doors, probably leading to the corridor and the bathroom. Patricia assumed the room had been modernized in that respect, at least.

She noticed her bags had been set in a corner under a wall hanging, and this drew her attention back to the tapestries and paintings, or rather what they depicted. Satyrs and nymphs, devils and damsels, griffins and gargoyles, naked, in various positions. The figures wrestled in an apocalyptic orgy of torture and sex, fire and brimstone.

This couldn't possibly be the room's original décor. Or, she amended, most of the furniture and even the depraved artwork may have been part and parcel of the great house's original inhabitants, William and Bess d'Arcy, when the first wing of the manor house was constructed in the mid-1500s. But certainly by the 1790s, when Fitzwilliam Darcy and Elizabeth Bennet had lived here, such furnishings would not have been tolerated. (Patricia was sure of this; she had first read *Pride and Prejudice* when she was a young girl, and reread it on the airplane to London after being contacted by Mr. Newell about the Pemberley legacy.)

It didn't bode well that the house's current inhabitants seemed to take after the debauched and corrupt sixteenth century d'Arcys, rather than their more refined descendents. One of Patricia's first acts as the new matriarch of Pemberley House would be to restore this room, and any others, to their rightful state.

She heard footsteps in the hallway outside her room, and for some reason she didn't want anyone to know she was up and investigating her room. Besides, her nightgown was sheer and the pinks of her nipples showed through. She climbed back into the wooden bed and pulled the covers up to her neck.

A rap came at the door.

"Come in," Patricia called, but the door opened before she was finished speaking. So much for privacy, she thought. I'll have to take a look at how, or if, that door locks.

Doctor Moran came in, followed by Richard and Carla Deguy. The doctor was in his mid-sixties, with greying hair, a paunch, and an old-fashioned walrus mustache. His nose and cheeks were red with broken blood vessels. He smiled at her, showing a mouthful of bad teeth.

"Good morning, Miss Wildman," the doctor said and he reintroduced himself. They had met the previous night but it had been hectic with the police there.

"Good morning," Patricia said. "This is quite a welcoming committee."

"Just wanted to make sure you were all right after that beastly night. We were all terribly worried, coz," Richard said. His manner, however, was offhand and belied his words of concern. She noticed his rather reptilian gaze lingering on her generous cleavage, and tugged the covers up higher.

Then Richard pulled chairs around the bed and took Carla's hand and guided her to the seat closest to Patricia.

"This is my sister, Carla."

Carla extended her hand and Patricia grasped it. A feathery tingle started in Patricia's fingertips, up her arms and shoulders, and raised the tiny hairs at the back of her neck. Carla wore a wraparound gauzy white blouse, a plaid miniskirt, and white stockings and thigh-high white go-go boots with thick heels. Unlike Patricia, she cared little if anyone realized she didn't wear a bra. Patricia noticed Carla's dark nipples under the blouse, which did little to keep her magnificent breasts in check. She also noticed that as Richard seated his sister in the chair by Patricia, his hand brushed and lingered on her backside before it grazed up her back and came to rest on her shoulder at the base of the neck.

Patricia did not have any siblings; perhaps Richard displayed what he considered normal brotherly affection. Carla did not seem to mind. Then Patricia noticed the telltale bulge in Richard's pants. She told herself to let it go, she wouldn't have to deal with him for very long.

"I'm very pleased to meet you at last, Patricia." Carla's voice was smooth and rich, like a cello. She held onto Patricia's hand and maintained eye contact for a long time, so long that Patricia became somewhat uncomfortable. "Your eyes are very beautiful. The gold flecks are unique. I've never seen anything like them."

"Thank you. And I'm pleased to meet you as well. I recognize you from your picture," Patricia said.

Richard and Doctor Moran also seated themselves, in a semicircle around Patricia's bed. "I'm sorry," Patricia said,

"I guess I must be a late riser. Am I late for breakfast? You all didn't have to come and greet me, though. I'll wash up and come downstairs."

Doctor Moran grinned. "Not at all, my dear, not at all. You've had a terrible time of it. Rest here as long as you wish."

"Yes, do. Breakfast, or lunch, or whatever, is whenever you want it," Carla said.

"Then…"

"The thing is, Patricia," Richard said, "we wanted to speak with you before you came down."

"Oh?"

"Yes, about the dowager. You see," Moran said, "she mustn't be told about last night, about the attack on you and Richard. We fear the excitement will be too much for her heart. She is 103 years old, you know."

"Yes, of course I know and of course I won't say anything. I would never want to upset her. But didn't she hear the commotion, the police here in the house, and ask about it?"

"No, the old lady sleeps through anything. Except she stays up all night, can't sleep she says, on the nights old Bess is supposed to come—"

"Richard, would you stop prattling on, please?" Carla said. But there was a tone of command in her voice. "Our cousin isn't interested in silly local superstitions, are you dear? Now, Patricia understands she isn't to mention the attack to the duchess, so let's leave her now and let her get dressed." Carla began to shoo the men out.

"Do you need a tranquilizer, my dear?" the doctor asked.

"What? No, of course not, I'm fine."

Doctor Moran continued to gaze at her with a kind, yet penetrating expression.

"Really. I'm fine, thank you. I don't want any drugs."

"Our coz Patricia is a tough one, eh? Nothing from Boots for her. Well, I'm off to find a tall glass, some ice, and four fingers. You coming, doc?"

"Richard, it's 11 o'clock in the morning."

"Yes, sis, and after last night, 11 o'clock seems like just the right time for a tall glass of bourbon. You want one too?" he called back as he and Doctor Moran exited Patricia's room, but clearly he didn't expect a reply.

Carla returned the chairs to their proper places. In the doorway, she looked back at Patricia in bed. "I can show you my closet later, maybe you'll see something you like. Do you want any help unpacking or picking out something to wear? I can help you dress, if you like."

"No, thank you. Was it you who got me out of my clothes and into bed?"

"Oh no, that was Miss Neston, the maid. I wouldn't have complained, mind you." Carla grinned, like a wolf. She cocked her hip sidewise in the doorway, which tugged the hem of the short skirt above the tops of her stockings, showing a couple inches of her white thighs.

Patricia realized then that Carla's lack of undergarments extended below the belt as well as above.

"It would have made me very happy to help you get situated last night. But I had another engagement. Maybe tonight?" Carla asked.

Patricia reddened at the proposition, and her voice caught.

Carla laughed.

"Patricia, you're very beautiful. Maybe you're the most beautiful girl I've ever seen. Your parents must have been exquisite. Anyway, I was just kidding with you. You mustn't take me seriously. You mustn't take any of us seriously. Now, enjoy a hot bath—I'll send Miss Neston up to draw it for you—and then get dressed and we'll see you downstairs." Carla waved and closed the door behind her.

Patricia bounded up out of bed, found the ancient lock, and secured it. The maid did come a few minutes later to prepare the bath and Patricia peeked out of the keyhole before letting her in. After Miss Neston left, Patricia luxuriated in the hot water; she felt an urgent need to clean off, both literally and figuratively, the filth from the previous night. She thought about the three inhabitants of Pemberley House she had met so far.

Richard Deguy was a lush. Although she still found him very handsome, in his resemblance to the actor Richard Greene, he was craven. She hadn't been impressed with his drunkenness when he picked her up at the train station, his carrying on with the barmaid Rosamond, and his cowardice at running away after the car crash. She doubted his claims that he had searched for her and her attackers. Yes, it was a pounding storm, but in retrospect Mary's Tower was an obvious place to look.

Patricia was fairly sure Richard would make a play for her soon, despite already having gotten Rosamond pregnant. Whereas Patricia had previously been attracted to him—or at least the picture of him she had seen before she met him, with its revealing bulge at the crotch—now he repelled her.

Doctor Moran seemed harmless, and she wondered how much medicine he actually practiced, living here as the dowager's personal physician. She knew he had given her a sedative the previous night, but she wouldn't let him prescribe anything else for her. Her father had been one of the world's leading medical men and she had no intention of allowing anyone less qualified than him, or her late husband Denis, or Doctor Miller, near her.

At least not near her in the medical sense.

And then there was Carla. While it was obvious Richard would sooner or later make an unwelcome advance, the sister had already done so. Or was it unwelcome? Patricia asked herself as she soaked in the foamy water. Well, it was, at least right now. Carla's timing was bad. Wasn't there something off, Patricia thought, about a woman who made a lesbian pass at another woman who had just been victimized and assaulted by a lesbian the night before? Or maybe the men hadn't told Carla about that part. Maybe they didn't think it was rape if it wasn't man-on-woman.

She decided to give Carla the benefit of the doubt, for now. And if she felt like it, maybe take her up on her offer. She had had one lesbian experience, with a friend, when she was younger. Actually, no thanks to Ernie, she had now had two such encounters. The thought soured her. Carla was attractive, more than attractive, in fact. But perhaps that wasn't enough, right now, to overcome the trauma of last night's attack. Patricia was confused, and still upset at her helplessness the previous night. She wasn't accustomed to helplessness, to being a victim. She didn't like it.

Maybe she wouldn't take Carla up on her proposal, after all.

Patricia gave up thinking about it, got out of the tub, dried off, dressed, and left her room to see Pemberley House.

8.

ORAN SHOWED PATRICIA around the estate. The dowager, he explained, and the grandchildren, Austin the chauffer, Doctor Moran, the housekeeper, the maid, and a butler lived in the private part of the house which was shut off from the public part, where visitors came by for public tours on weekdays. Guides took care of the public side, and there was an extensive cleaning and grounds staff, but it was for the most part separate except that Richard and Carla administered the public side.

The doctor showed her around the grounds surrounding the house. On all sides, the great mansion was bordered by a vast park of lawn and gardens, surrounded by the huge oak trees of Pemberley Woods. The house itself was a large stone building of several stories, peppered with tall windows, French doors leading to the portico which surrounded the building (or on higher levels to narrow balconies with wrought iron railings), and cupolas and turrets. The original manor house, Moran told Patricia, was first built in the mid-1500s. Additions had been made over the ensuing centuries, and rebuilding had occurred when a fire had destroyed a portion of the house in the seventeenth century. Mary's Tower, where Patricia had been taken last night, dated from the 1580s, shortly after the death of Bess of Pemberley. It was up on a hill behind Pemberley House, and it was said that Mary, Queen of Scots, had spent some time there.

Next Doctor Moran and Patricia crossed a small bridge over a stream and he took her in through the vast entrance hall, through rooms lined with priceless and superb works of art, including countless statues and paintings from different eras. Her father had emphasized art and music as well as the sciences in her education—in fact he was an accomplished violinist—and she recognized works by several great painters, among them Rembrandt, Hallward, Picasso, Scarletin, and the Frenchman Horace Vernet. Not for the first time, she wondered if her late husband Denis Verner was distantly related to the French painter. One of her father's tutors in criminology—some said the world's greatest detective—had been related to Vernet. Her father, and therefore she, had also been a distant relative of the Great Detective. Thus, perhaps she had been very distantly related to her husband. Not closely enough in degree to make their relationship incestuous, not like Richard and Carla, if Richard and Carla were actually having sex.

It didn't matter any more, anyway. Denis and her father and mother were all dead and she was alone.

Moran next showed Patricia the magnificent dining-parlour, a large, well-proportioned room with a pleasing aspect looking back out onto the park and a lake and Pemberley Woods. The rooms were lofty, the furnishings elegant, and Patricia felt relieved that overall the house was handsome and did not emulate the *outré* decoration of her guest room, but rather retained the graceful and tasteful spirit it must have had in the day when Mr. and Mrs. Fitzwilliam Darcy held the estate.

Then Moran took her down the Great Hall of Pemberley House. The side to their left was covered with a gallery of portraits, large and small, while the right side had massive windows that allowed the sunlight to flow in like golden honey. She imagined Lizzy Bennet touring the same hall almost 200 years ago with Mr. and Mrs. Gardiner, conducted by Pemberley's housekeeper, and envisaging herself the mistress of Pemberley.

Moran steered her to one painting in particular. It was a handsome portrait of Fitzwilliam Darcy and Elizabeth Bennet themselves, painted shortly after their courtship and marriage. Happiness, integrity, and prosperity practically leaped off the canvas. A later portrait showed the Darcys with their son, Fitzwilliam Bennet Darcy. Moran described the next portrait as that of the son and his wife, Agatha Jansenius.

Next Moran led her to the picture of her great-grandfather. He was tall man with a red beard, a hooked nose, and piercing grey eyes.

"William Cecil Clayton, the sixth Duke of Greystoke. He died in 1909." Patricia was startled. Richard had come up beside them without her noticing. Either she was so engrossed in the various depictions of her family that she wasn't paying attention, or he was stealthier than she would have credited him. Or both. At any rate, his presence was not entirely welcome to Patricia, but he didn't seem to notice. He carried on, sipping at the generous bourbon he carried in his right hand. The latter was un-English, but since bourbon was not easy to get in England, Patricia guessed he must have disliked Scotch.

"What a wonderful array of paintings, d'Arcys and Darcys and Claytons," Richard said. "Of course, your grandfather and father are not among them."

Patricia knew her grandfather and father were of a line considered illegitimate. She didn't need Richard Deguy to tell her that. In an effort to change the subject and still remain pleasant, Patricia asked Doctor Moran, "How did the sixth duke—my great-grandfather—come to possess Pemberley House after the Darcys? It's my understanding that I count both the Darcys and the Claytons among my ancestors."

"That's true," Moran replied. "Let's move down a bit farther and I'll show you some of the older paintings, the d'Arcys. This is William d'Arcy, the first Baron of Lambton."

"The madman I told you about last night, coz," Richard interjected, and Patricia had to admit, looking at the baron's cruel countenance framed between the coronet's six silver balls and the

Elizabethan collar, that the artist had captured the gleam of lunacy in the baron's eyes.

"Next to him is his wife Bess d'Arcy, or Bess of Pemberley," Moran said. "It sounds like Richard here has already filled your head with ghost stories about Bess."

"Yes," Patricia said. She noticed Bess resembled Carla quite a bit.

"William murdered Bess in 1570, the day their daughter Jane d'Arcy was born. He later also slit Jane's throat just as he had Bess's, on her twenty-second birthday, and was finally committed to the madhouse. Jane's older brother, Christopher d'Arcy—here's a picture of him—was left to carry on the line. One of his descendents, Ursula d'Arcy, married Ralph Arthur Caldwell-Grebson. There's their family portrait. Your great-grandfather, the sixth Duke of Greystoke, was descended from Ralph and Ursula."

"Then this so-called Pemberley Curse, which was enacted when Jane was murdered and passed on through Christopher and his descendants…" Patricia mused. "My great-grandfather was also subject to it?"

"If one believes the legend, yes," Moran said. "But Richard, you mustn't pester her with these ghost stories. We don't want to scare her off."

Richard shrugged.

"I'm not scared," Patricia said.

"That's the spirit," Richard said, and he chuckled.

Moran shook his head, and took Patricia by the elbow. He led her farther down the Hall and indicated another portrait. "This is Sir Gawain Darcy. He purchased Pemberley from Fitzwilliam Bennet Darcy when the latter underwent a period of economic hardship. Later on, your great-grandfather purchased the estate from Sir Gawain, keeping it in the family, as it were."

He took her back down to the end of the Great Hall near where they had entered. "This is Edith, Duchess of Greystoke. Now the Dowager Duchess," he amended. The painting showed her as a woman of thirty. She was beautiful, with a straight mouth over a little chin, aquiline-nose, dark-eyes, with dark eyebrows.

A forceful character showed in her portrait. "She was originally Edith Jansenius, of a rich, Christianized Jewish family."

At Patricia's sharp look, Moran nodded. "Yes, very good. Edith Jansenius was the niece of Agatha Jansenius, who married Fitzwilliam Bennet Darcy. Fitzwilliam and Agatha's daughters, Edith's cousins, were Athena and Delhi Darcy. As I said, all in the family. Here we are, this is the wedding portrait of Athena and her husband, the fifth Duke of Greystoke. Their son, John Clayton, predeceased his father by a few months.[3] Thus, when the fifth duke perished, the title passed to his younger brother, your great-grandfather."

Patricia nodded and then moved back to the portrait of Edith, Duchess of Greystoke. "How do you and Carla fit in all this?" she asked Richard.

"The duchess took in father years ago. She was traveling in Italy and became friends with a couple at a resort in Palermo. They were killed in an accident and she adopted their son, our father. She outlived him," he said, and raised his glass to his lips once more. "Perhaps she'll outlive us all."

"I see," Patricia said.

She also saw a strong resemblance between the Deguy twins and the duchess' portrait. Perhaps she imagined it. She took a long look at Richard Deguy again.

He smirked at her and said, "Enough dawdling among the ancestors, now, Patricia. She's ready to see you."

| 9.

RICHARD LED PATRICIA and Doctor Moran to meet the duchess in her hothouse rooms, essentially an indoor garden lush with vegetation and humidity. "Aren't you coming in?" Patricia asked Richard.

"No, no, you and the doc'll do fine without me." He held up his empty glass and winked. "I'm off to find a refill."

Moran showed Patricia to a wicker chair, pulled one up for himself next to the old lady, and presented Patricia.

"I'm pleased to meet you, Your Grace," Patricia said, using the honorific as she had been instructed by the lawyer Mr. Newell.

"Yes, yes, of course you are," the dowager replied. "Come to gawk at the old woman who's outlived everyone, have you?"

Patricia was nonplussed. "But, Your Grace sent for me."

"Only because manners called for it, Miss Wildman." Then the dowager's mouth turned up a little. "I'm just having you on, dear. I can do that, I'm old."

Moran laughed and took the old lady's hand. Patricia watched; she expected him to release it as the little joke passed, but he held on, leaving his hand in hers, both hands resting in her lap.

The duchess was less feeble than Patricia expected; she was still sharp and obviously her mind was good. She was 103, but looked perhaps 85, and even so Patricia could see the remnants of her youthful beauty.

"I'll come straight to the point, young lady. I wish your assurance you'll take good care of my grandchildren. I mean the children of my adopted son. But I treat them as I would my own flesh and blood."

"With all due respect, Your Grace, I'm not sure I'll accept the inheritance. And Mr. Newell tells me most of the estate except Pemberley House itself will be sold to pay death taxes."

"Indeed! We shall see, we shall just see." The duchess turned to Moran. "Augustus, get me a drink. I think Miss Wildman and I are going to have a long chat."

"You really shouldn't. Your heart—"

"Augustus. Bring me some wine."

Moran mumbled something and wandered back inside the main house.

"Have you known Doctor Moran long," Patricia asked; Mr. Newell, had briefed her on Moran, but she was making polite conversation.

"What? Of course I've known him a long time. I'm 103. I've known everyone a long time."

Patricia reddened. "I only meant…That is, what I meant to say is, has the doctor been with you a long time, in your service at Pemberley House, or is he a more recent addition to your household."

The duchess gave Patricia a grin, which made her parchment-like skin fold and crinkle and pull tight against her skull, showing blue veins. Patricia thought the grin made the old woman look somewhat terrifying.

"Child, I have known Augustus Moran practically since he was born, and he has serviced me from the first day he joined the staff here as my private secretary."

Patricia wasn't sure how to take that, and she was a little bit sickened. Surely Moran was almost 40 years her junior. She couldn't really mean…Then Moran came back with the duchess' wine and she fussed at him for bringing only half a glass.

While they quarreled like old lovers—at least that's how Patricia saw it now, based on the duchess' comment—Patricia thought, My God, this woman was born four years after the Civil War ended; she lived under Queen Victoria's reign for 32 years; she remembers first-hand Gladstone and Disraeli, Bismarck, and the famous around-the-world trip of Phileas Fogg; she was sixteen years old when the first automobile with an internal combustion engine was made, and she could conceivably live for another seven or so years.

"Miss Wildman. Miss Wildman."

Patricia startled out of her reverie.

"I asked you about your parents," the duchess said. "I understand they were of better character than your grandfather."

"I didn't know grandfather," Patricia said. "He died almost 20 years before I was born. Father did speak highly of him, though."

"That is to be expected, is it not?"

"Yes, I suppose. And...father did grow up in a rather strange environment."

"How so?"

"Well, his mother died very soon after he was born, and after that he was raised by a succession of tutors and scientists. It was necessary, though. Grandfather was a great explorer, always traveling. He penetrated the wilds of Hidalgo, met previously undiscovered tribes of the Maya, and even mounted an expedition to the fabled Maple White Land in South America."

"It sounds like a very unhappy childhood. One could almost say your father had been abandoned."

Patricia flushed. "It wasn't like that at all. Father's upbringing was unique. He had mentors all over the world, experts in chemistry, medicine, biology. He studied with some of the greatest detectives who ever lived, like Sherlock Holmes and Craig Kennedy. Indian *fakirs* taught him to alter his appearance by adding or subtracting from his height. He even studied with masters of disguise, so he could infiltrate the criminal element and defeat them from within. It was all a program grandfather devised. He wanted father to be the greatest crime fighter who ever lived, and he succeeded. He was a superman."

The duchess raised an eyebrow. "Calm yourself, my child."

The old lady was right, and Patricia was embarrassed. "I'm sorry. I get a little worked up about father. I didn't mean anything."

"I'm sure that's true," the dowager said. "Of course, you didn't mention that your father also studied with some of the greatest thieves of all time. All in the name of getting inside the criminal mind, of course, or at least that's how your grandfather would have justified exposing his son to such men."

"What do you know about it?" Patricia was no longer embarrassed, but was angry now.

"More than you think. Your father visited here once, and while I had admiration for how he handled himself on that occasion, I made it a point to keep abreast of his activities and investigate him further. You left out that when he was a boy, he studied with Arsène Lupin, perhaps the greatest ever of the so-called gentleman thieves."

Patricia said nothing.

"I asked you about your mother. You've gone strangely quiet now, young lady. Perhaps it's because much later your father ended up marrying Lupin's daughter, a girl more than half his age? A girl who took after her notorious father?"

Patricia was defensive again. "Father was always young for his age. And besides, mother was reformed. Father was a great doctor and helped her overcome her inclination toward crime."

"And then he married one of his own patients. That hardly seems—"

"Who are you, of all people, to judge? She was cured, she was no longer his patient. And they were in love, something you—"

"Enough," the duchess commanded, and Patricia got control of herself. "You were about to say that I could know little of love? Perhaps. Perhaps not.

"In any case, your pedigree is mixed. Your father was to be generally admired, your mother less so." Patricia burned at this attack on her mother, which probably struck home even harder because it was nothing she hadn't thought of herself.

However, she said nothing as the duchess continued: "Your grandfather, however, was the worst of the lot, and thus genetics are stacked against you. I cannot see how you are qualified to take possession of this house and its great legacy."

They sat in silence for a while, beads of moisture rolling down Patricia's forehead. She breathed deeply of the muggy hothouse air, sucking the scent of decaying plant matter and loam into her lungs.

The duchess looked at Patricia equably, as if she had not just greatly insulted her. The doctor also sat still, a slight leer marring his thin lips. Patricia realized he might not be quite as harmless or doddering as she had thought.

When she regained control of her emotions, Patricia said, "You're being dramatic. Next you'll ask, 'Are the shades of Pemberley to be thus polluted?' Just what is it you have against my grandfather, anyway?"

"Is it possible you don't know? Your father never told you?"

Patricia shrugged. "I'm asking."

"It happened while I was…estranged from my husband. Your great-grandfather, the sixth duke."

"Why did you leave?"

"Your grandfather, of course. He was in the house. He wasn't acknowledged as my husband's son. That wouldn't have been proper. But he was here, all the time, serving as my husband's private secretary. He knew he would not inherit and was jealous. It was untenable. I left for the Continent. And while I was gone, your grandfather, James Wildman, repaid the kindnesses shown to him by joining the innkeeper Hayes in a plot to kidnap his own half-brother, Arthur. My son! My poor, poor son. In the course of events, a German master named Heidegger was murdered. My husband called in Sherlock Holmes from London to solve the mystery. Even then, after the truth came out, my husband protected James, helping him get out of the country and on his way to a new life, supposedly in Australia. He should have hung along with Hayes." The old lady shook with venom.

"Still, James was gone, that's what mattered, and with his departure my husband persuaded me to return from southern

France and reconcile. Although later we learned that the cad had been secretly married and dragged his young pregnant wife halfway across the world with him when he ran off Down Under. I said 'we.' I should have said my husband. I cared not a whit what happened to the scoundrel."

Patricia was shocked. However, the story explained a lot. Her father, James Wildman, Jr., had had only good and positive things to say about his own father. Wildman Sr. had made his fortune in Australia and in the Klondike gold rush and hunting around the world for diverse treasures. Although the senior Wildman's wife, Arronaxe Larsen, had died at a very young age, he had done more than his best to raise his son as a man of integrity, honor, and justice. Patricia could see now that Wildman Sr. was driven by guilt and shame to atone for what he had done to his younger half-brother.

However, she didn't say any of this to the dowager. What good would it do? Seventy-two years later, and the old lady was still trembling with anger. Her own son, William Cecil Arthur Clayton, who had been kidnapped as a young boy, was now dead and gone. As for Patricia, the grandfather she had never met was dead. Her parents were dead.

What did it matter?

"I'm sorry for your loss, and your pain," Patricia told the old woman.

The duchess' rheumy eyes filled with tears. "Arthur was never the same after that. In his late teens he went on an African expedition, and I never saw him again. He married in 1910, to an American woman from Baltimore, and never brought his wife here to present her to me. When in England, he spent all his time at his estate in Cumberland County in northern England or in London. I even tried to surprise him several times in Cumberland or London with unannounced visits, but he always managed to evade me, to not be there. And any agents or detectives I sent were stonewalled. But he spent the greater part of his time at his estate in British East Africa, anyway."

"Once," Moran interjected, "Her Grace even received a visit from the world's richest man, James D. Stonecraft—"

"That was back in '17, I think. He was richer than the Rockefellers, at that time anyway."

"Stonecraft was interested in the duchess' son and offered to help her in her quest to see him. But nothing came of it…"

"Arthur never again set foot in his home, Pemberley House, from when he first left for Africa until I received word a few months ago that he and his wife were dead…No children[4]… Something happened in that jungle that changed him forever."

The duchess rambled, speaking to the air. Then her old black eyes burned, and her hand, clawed and twisted with age, gripped Patricia's wrist.

"Now you understand, don't you? My son, dead to me all those years. It doesn't matter that he truly died just a few months ago. And my adopted son, Carlo. Dead. My grandchildren Richard and Carla are all I have left, all I have, and I will not see them put out, you understand? Do you understand me?" The old lady was in a frenzy now, spittle flying from her cracked lips. She shuddered a little, and Moran wrapped his arms around her, whispered at her to calm down.

"Duchess, please, it's time for your rest, time to rest now." He rocked the dowager back and forth, and looked up at Patricia. "I trust you can find your own way back, Miss Wildman?"

Patricia took the not-so-subtle hint. She left.

10.

PATRICIA STRODE THROUGH the maze of Elizabethan corridors and lavish rooms of Pemberley. At length she found herself again in the Great Hall. Outside the huge windows, the sunny day was gone and black clouds were piling up. The wind shook the dark Derbyshire countryside and a gloom settled over the tall tors in the distance.

"Lost?"

Richard had come up behind her.

She nodded. "A little."

"I'll take you back to your room."

Patricia's chamber had been made up by Miss Neston, her clothing hung up, and her personal items stored in the bathroom.

"All tidied up for Bess's coming tonight, I see," Richard remarked.

"Tonight?"

"Yes, at midnight. Remember? This is the first of three night's running that the ghost will appear. Perfect room for it, too."

"What do you mean?"

"Why coz, this was Bess's room. Left pretty close to how it was in her day, too, I think."

"Bess's room!" Patricia said. "Why didn't anyone tell me before?"

"Well, the timing wasn't right last night, and this is the first time it's come up, I suppose. What's the problem, anyway, it's just an old superstition."

"Yes, you're right, of course. Richard, I'm tired. I'm going to nap, now. I'll come back down later."

"Right you are, Patricia. Get caught up on your rest." He raised his glass slightly and closed the door behind him.

Patricia went to the door and turned the key in the lock. Then she crossed the room to the four-poster bed and lay down, falling asleep soon after her head hit the pillow. She dreamed of Denis, and he made love to her.

She woke, refreshed, and for a moment in the mist of waking she didn't know where she was. Denis' face morphed into Richard's, or was it Carla's, with some tinge of Ernie's?

She was repulsed. If she ever saw Ernie again…Her father could never have been accused of being a non-violent man, but he avoided killing his enemies if at all possible. Would he have been as dispassionate about the attack on his daughter? He had trained her in his philosophy, his own moral code.

What would she do if she ever encountered Ernie again?

Patricia showered and went downstairs in response to the summons for tea. Richard and Carla were in the sitting room. Carla poured tea for herself and Patricia from an old and ornate silver service. Richard drank bourbon.

"Sleep well, coz? Hope your slumber wasn't disturbed with dreams of Bess," Richard said.

"No, I slept fine, thanks. I didn't dream about Bess."

"Patricia, Richard and I were just discussing the duchess when you came down. What did you think of her?" Carla asked.

"She seems like a complex woman," Patricia said. "I guess it would be hard not to be after living so long."

"I think you're right," Carla said. "The duchess has been hinting around to Richard and me there's something she'd like to confess before she dies, but may leave it to be revealed in her private papers to be opened after her death. Richard and I were just speculating about what it could be. Any ideas?"

"None. You'd be in a much better position to guess than I. But I imagine someone her age has any number of secrets. They may be important to her but turn out to be completely innocent and harmless to us."

"Oh, don't be a spoilsport, Patricia. I'm absolutely wild about these ancient scandals." Carla had grabbed her hand and, as she continued to speak, neglected to release it.

"Listen. Maybe it was her affair with Edward, Prince of Wales. The duchess has never mentioned it, but I heard it from an eighty-year-old friend of the duchess, who heard it from her mother. The duchess was first married at age sixteen to the Marquess Blackwater and apparently had an affair with the Prince of Wales. Her husband found out about it somehow and died of a broken heart, some say; others say it was a hushed-up suicide. Then she married the sixth duke."

"And you think this is what she wants to tell you?"

"I'm not sure. It all occurred so long ago and surely nobody would think less of the duchess now. Besides, she isn't really Victorian, she's pretty liberal and modern in many things."

"As I understand it, some husbands were complicit, or at least looked the other way, in their wives' affairs with Prince Edward."

"That's true." Richard joined the conversation, chuckling. "But old Marquess Blackie didn't even have to look the other way. The whole affair began and ended before he even married the duchess. When he found out, it seems he couldn't stand the thought his young bride wasn't as virginal as he thought when he married her. Blew his brains right out of his skull."

"How did he find out?" Patricia asked.

"Found some love letters, it's said, and that's all it took," Richard said.

"I suppose the shame might be enough to haunt the duchess, even after all this time," Patricia said.

Carla grinned and squeezed Patricia's hand. "I don't think so. Like I said, the duchess isn't all that Victorian in her behavior and attitudes. Isn't that right, Richard?"

"Right you are, sis." The two siblings shared a knowing look. It was brief, but Patricia caught it and it annoyed her. "We know she had many admirers after the sixth duke's death, and she spent a lot of time on the Continent. She was not celibate."

Carla giggled. "Of course not. I once found a packet of letters she had left on her desk. Most were from the 1910s and '20s. She was quite the modern woman. Famous artists, writers, captains of industry, they were all eager to woo her. Once she took a French vicomte as her lover. She even had a fling with some big game hunter—Helmson, I think the name was—in Paris before he left on a big expedition to Africa."

Richard still laughed along with his sister, and Patricia thought he was half-loaded. She also didn't care much for the gossip and the I've-got-a-secret game that Richard and Carla seemed to be playing with her.

"It looks like the storms have cleared up a little. I think I'll go for a walk." Patricia disengaged her hand from Carla's and stood up.

"We'll go along," Carla said.

"Yes, coz. A breath of fresh air'll do, but don't forget the poachers. You shouldn't walk around the grounds alone."

Patricia had to admit that made sense and shrugged in acquiescence.

They strolled in silence around the lake, Carla and Richard walking somewhat behind Patricia and to her right. She thought about the two siblings. Something was a bit off about them, as if they were reflections in a funhouse mirror. But what was it? Richard was a drunk, but many people were. She felt there was something vaguely dangerous about him, but perhaps that was just her distrust magnified, based on his disappearing act after they were attacked the previous night.

Carla seemed better put together than her brother, more capable. If anything, she was the dominant of the two, with Richard following her lead. But Patricia couldn't understand people like Carla, who would unabashedly talk about family matters and history better left to discretion. If the duchess wanted to share her secrets with Patricia, that was one thing. It was another thing altogether to hear the duchess' grandchildren—even adopted grandchildren—as they blithely discussed her sex life with a virtual stranger. Patricia was no prude. The twins' behavior was unseemly. At least, it didn't fit in with her preconceived notions of refined English conduct and manners which she had expected to encounter at Pemberley.

Nor had she expected Richard to receive oral sex from a barmaid while chauffeuring Patricia to Pemberley, to constantly leer at her, and to feel up his own sister. Or for Carla to make a pass at her. Everyone here had sex on the brain. Including her, she admitted, although she hadn't had much time, or inclination, she realized now, to obsess over her father since she'd arrived.

But she did wonder why she'd been consumed with thoughts of sex, lately.

"I do hope you're feeling better, Miss Wildman?"

The deep voice startled Patricia out of her thoughts and she realized the gamekeeper, whom she recognized from the previous evening when the police had come to the house, had joined them at the water's edge.

"Yes, thank you."

"We weren't properly introduced last evening, I'm afraid. I'm Mr. Parker."

"Patricia Wildman." Oblivious to English class distinctions, she extended her hand, and Parker took it. She felt the same sort of tingle that she had when she had touched Carla's hand. She could tell he admired and was attracted to her. However, unlike Richard's reptilian gaze undressing her with his eyes, Parker's expression was open and friendly, with light blue-grey eyes and ash-blonde hair. He had an aura of quiet strength which reminded her of her father.

Putting Richard up next to Parker, she couldn't imagine how she ever could have thought Richard attractive. He still had the Richard Greene good looks she had first seen in the photograph Mr. Newell had sent, but in person there was something dark and dead behind his eyes.

"That's Lady Wildman to you, Parker," Richard said.

"Oh, no, Patricia is fine. Besides, as I told the duchess earlier today, I haven't even decided if I'll accept the inheritance or not. So please, I'd prefer first names. Chalk it up to my vulgar American manners, if you must." Patricia smiled at Richard.

"Fine by me. I'm Pete then. First name is Charles, but my friends use my middle name," Parker said, returning the smile.

"How droll," Richard said. "Any progress on tracking down the poachers, Pete?"

"None, I'm afraid, although the police suspect that the two, Ernie and Jack, who attacked Miss Wildman—sorry, Patricia—last night may not have been the poachers who've been about the grounds. Not sure what puts them of that mind, except no other reports on the poachers have included a woman among them."

Patricia thought about Ernie and Jack. The mention of Ernie brought front and center her memories of the previous night's assault. It wasn't the lesbian intercourse that traumatized or shocked her; she was too responsive for that. She belonged to a new generation, many of whom were more sexually free, even if her father was a rigid, moral person—too rigid, perhaps, because of the training by her grandfather, who had overreacted in his repentance of his criminal activity.

And it wasn't even the first time Patricia had had a lesbian encounter. She had been with a good friend a few years ago, when she was fifteen. Helen Benson was a few years older than Patricia, and her family regularly came to visit the Wildmans. Helen's father was a noted crime fighter in the late 1930s and '40s. Her mother was the former Ellen Patrick, who had also had a career fighting crime several decades back in the guise of "The Domino Lady." Helen's parents married in the late '40s after her father finally confirmed his first wife and child were really dead. Ellen provided a light and playful touch to the otherwise grim crime fighter's life.

On one visit, Patricia and Helen had been in her room. The parents were out for the evening and the girls were listening to The Beatles' *Revolver* and smoking pot that Helen had brought with her. Patricia had never smoked marijuana before, and although she knew her father would disapprove—he neither smoked nor drank alcohol—she also knew his disapproval would not emanate from any arbitrary moral judgment, but rather from the fact that she was polluting her body and ceding mental control for the time she was under the influence of the drug. As much as she loved her father, and as much as she excelled at the training program he had devised for her, she did not always share his discipline and his rigid lifestyle. In that way she took after her mother.

So she had smoked the joint Helen had offered to her. And under the droning, psychedelic rhythm of "Tomorrow Never Knows," Helen had seduced her, starting by kissing her neck and ears, and then moving down to her round, full breasts. Before she knew it, Helen had gently slid off Patricia's lacy panties, and buried herself between Patricia's long legs, bobbing her head up and down, flicking her tongue in and out, up and down and around in tiny, insistent circles.

Patricia was not a virgin. She had lost her virginity the year before to the son of one of her mother's best friends, an English boy named Clive. Clive and his mother, Violet Holmes, were also frequent visitors to the Wildmans' upstate New York enclave. Apparently Violet and Patricia's mother had been quite a team back in the late '40s, and they regaled Patricia and Clive with exploits that sometimes rivaled those of Patricia's father.

Clive's late father, Charles Reston, had been an agent for the Diogenes Club; one of the least known and most eccentric arms of the British Secret Service, it dealt with matters unfathomable and *outré*. Reston had been killed in Oran, during one of Adélaïde and Violet's first adventures; it was, in fact, the case that marked the very first meeting of Adélaïde Lupin and Doctor James Clarke Wildman.

Clive liked to intimate his father was alive and serving as one of England's most ruthless yet glamorous secret agents. Patricia dismissed this as a harmless fantasy, and finding that it actually added to Clive's charms, had succumbed to his attentions during her fourteenth summer.

But the orgasm she experienced with Helen the following year was nothing like what it had been like with Clive. Or even when she masturbated and fantasized about her father.

Patricia had been raised to avoid ethnocentric judgments, that is, to be as non-judgmental about non-Western cultures and practices as it is possible for a human being to be. Still, as a woman, she was never so grateful, as she was at that moment, that she was not subject to tribal customs of female circumcision, which she couldn't help but regard as a form of mutilation.

She had also been grateful her parents had not been home to hear her loud cries of pleasure with Helen Benson.

So what troubled Patricia about the memories of Ernie wasn't the sex itself, but the situation and the loss of control. She hated Ernie for what she had done to her and intended to pay her back if she ever saw her again. This was another way, she realized, that she was different from her father, who was not driven by, or at least didn't act on, feelings of revenge.

Her mother, on the other hand, would have been entirely comfortable taking an eye for an eye. It was a point in common she had with her mother, which she hadn't recognized until now.

And why not? Ernie and Jack were criminals, and as far as Patricia was concerned, after what they had done to her, they didn't deserve any soft treatment.

But if they weren't the poachers, then what did they want? She did remember, now that they were discussing Jack and Ernie and the attack, Jack had mentioned something to the effect that he, "Couldn't find him, he ran off into the woods." Since Jack could have only meant the driver of the Rolls—Richard—she decided not to mention this in front of Richard and Carla. She wouldn't put it past Richard to be involved in something shady.

On the other hand, Richard had mentioned he had only driven because the chauffer, Austin, had been lamed in a previous attack by the poachers.

"That's fascinating, Pete," Richard was saying. "What vast progress you've made."

"Oh Richard, don't be such a bastard," Carla said.

"Well, I doubt any poachers are about in the daytime, because there are police and visitors around. The two kidnappers are either long gone or holed-up," Parker said.

The four walked on a bit in silence, until they came to a court-yard bordered by the house on one side and a freestanding garage on the other, backed by a high brick wall which connected the two. A tough looking man in chauffer's livery worked in the garage. He was little, dark, and scarred. He eyed Patricia and her companions as they passed.

"That's Austin, the bloke who was supposed to pick you up from London yesterday," Richard informed Patricia. "He's an ex-convict, taken on by Doctor Moran."

Speak of the devil. "What did he do?" she asked.

"Robbery."

"Isn't the duchess concerned?"

"The duchess? Not her. Moran told her of Austin's background and she wasn't worried a bit. In fact, she often talks to him, and loves to hear of his criminal exploits. The old girl has a criminal streak in her."

The four walked a bit further, Patricia and Parker ahead of the Deguy twins. When they reached the end of the lake, Richard and Carla parted ways with Patricia with Parker.

"We'll leave you two lovebirds alone, then," Richard said. "Take good care of Patricia, Pete. We wouldn't want anything to happen to her, would we? Especially after last night." Richard's smile and good cheer didn't make it to his eyes.

Carla rolled her eyes.

"I'll watch over the Lady, not to worry, sir," Parker replied.

Patricia could hear Carla laying into Richard as they walked away, calling him an ass. His protests faded as they disappeared from view.

"She's right, you know," Parker said.

"What?"

"Miss Deguy. She called her brother an ass."

Patricia laughed. "Yes, he is, isn't he?"

After walking around the grounds for another hour, past the lake, over small trickling streams, and through thick copses of forest growth, Patricia and Parker arrived at the ruins of Mary's Tower. It was surrounded by great oaks now, but in the old days, being up on a hill and from the top of the Tower, one could see quite a lot. In fact, one still could, through the trees.

They climbed to the top and sat in silence for a bit and watched the sun sink toward the horizon.

"Are you sure you're all right, being here?" Parker asked. "I mean, the attack..."

Patricia brushed it off. She was somewhat annoyed. "I'm fine. I'm not a China doll. I'll be fine."

"Sorry about that."

"It's okay. It's just that everyone is alternately fawning over me or trying to creep me out. Sometimes I almost think the fawning is a backdoor attempt to scare me. Oh, poor Patricia, be careful to not get attacked again. Watch out for Austin, Patricia, he's an ex-con. Look out for the poachers, Patricia! Don't be afraid of the ghost, Patricia, it's just a silly old legend, after all, ha, ha." She laughed and made spooky gestures, waving her fingers and arms in front of her. "Ooo, ooo, the ghost of Bess lives in your room, Patricia, she's going to get you."

Parker laughed with her. "Okay, okay. I'm sorry. No more China doll treatment for you, young miss. I can see you'll have no trouble running things around here."

"Well, I'm not sure I'll take it."

"What? After you just got done claiming you're not going to be scared off?"

"I'm not scared," she said. "But accepting this legacy is a big step. I'm still thinking about it."

"What's there to think about?"

"Running this estate is a big responsibility, I imagine. Plus, I wouldn't just inherit the house and grounds." Patricia was thinking about the duchess' admonition to take care of Richard and Carla. She wasn't even sure she'd accept the Pemberley legacy when she'd arrived yesterday, and the prospect of life under the same roof with

Richard and Carla didn't do much to encourage her. Or at least Richard. She was still evaluating Carla.

"How so?" asked Parker.

"In essence, I'd be inheriting all the people here. Carla and Richard, Doctor Moran, Austin and the other staff…"

"You have a problem with the staff here at Pemberley, Lady Wildman?" Parker said with mock offense.

Patricia saw the twinkle in his eye and knew he was kidding her.

"Absolutely. Take the grounds, for instance. Abominable. Atrocious, in fact. For instance, look over there. There, through that thicket. Those trees and bushes are obviously not properly cultivated. Completely unacceptable."

"Well, it is early spring, after all—"

"And there," she pointed at another area of the great woods, "the maintenance of that…Pete, look, what is that?"

"Well, your Ladyship—"

"No, I'm serious. I think there's someone down there." She continued pointing, directing his attention to a small clearing in an otherwise thick grove of old oaks.

Parker squinted. "I do believe you're right, Patricia. Two someones, in fact."

"What are they doing?"

"I think…" Parker colored. "That is, as far as I can tell, they are…It appears they're…*in flagrante*, as it were…"

"Yes, you're right. It's Richard and his barmaid. Having sex." She made a face. "Aren't there enough bedrooms in the house for that?"

"I imagine there are, but I doubt the duchess welcomes the girl with open arms."

"Of course not. Still…" Patricia looked at him. "*In flagrante*? That's pretty lofty for a mere groundskeeper. If I do decide to stay on here, you'll need to learn your place."

He returned her look. "And where would that be, your Ladyship?"

Now it was Patricia's turn to be embarrassed. "We'll talk about that, if and when the time comes."

"You're right." Parker stood up. "And as much as I'm enjoying this banter, I need to go over there and run them off."

"What? No, please, just leave it alone."

"I can't. I'm in charge of the grounds, remember? Besides, they might scare the wildlife, and we can't have that. C'mon, I'm not leaving you alone. You can stand over to the side a bit where they can't see you and I'll roust them off. After they're gone, I'll walk you back to the house."

"Richard will be furious. Won't he dismiss you?"

"Only the duchess can do that. She's as lecherous as her grandchildren, but I doubt Richard wants her to know about his escapades. Let's go."

11.

ATRICIA HAD THOUGHT dinner would never end.
Outside, black storm clouds had returned,
bringing with them peals of thunder and lightning.
The high French windows of the dining-parlour rattled as rain
pounded against the leaded crystal panes.

Inside, the duchess held court at the head of the table. Doctor
Moran sat to her left. Next to Moran was Carla. On the opposite
side sat Richard, with Patricia next to him.

The silver, China, and crystal were ancient and priceless. The food
was exquisite, the service impeccable, and the company distasteful.

Richard started out mentioning the ghost of Bess again. "This is
the first night, you know. First of three nights she'll appear at midnight."

"Richard, do be quiet," the duchess said. "You know I can't
sleep when Bess comes."

"But duchess, I can't do anything about that. Maybe the doc
can give you something to help you sleep. Besides, I've never understood why Bess upsets you. How exactly could you be related
to the ancient d'Arcys, anyway? And if you're not related, nothing
to worry about, right?"

Richard took a liberal drink of bourbon, then continued. "Now
our American cousin, here. She's related, no doubt about it. What
will you do when the ghost comes tonight, Patricia?"

"Not that I believe your tall stories, but what is anyone supposed to do when Bess allegedly appears?"

"Doc Moran can answer that, can't you Doc? He's the expert on the whole family." Richard turned to Moran. "So, Doc, how does one appease Bess, anyway?"

The old man tugged at his walrus moustache. "I have no intention of fostering these ridiculous legends."

"Aw, c'mon Doc. Patricia is put up in old Bess's room. Least you can do is let her in on how to deal with Bess when she, ahem, comes."

"Enough!"

The discussion halted at the duchess' command. The dining-parlour was dim, lit only by a few silver candelabra, but all could see she was white and shaking.

Richard was contrite. "Sorry about that, it's just—"

"Richard. Shut up," Carla said. "Now."

Meanwhile, Moran had moved his chair closer to the duchess and taken her trembling hand. He soothed her, speaking into her ear. The old lady was still pale, but her shallow breathing began to return to normal.

Moran moved away a little, but continued to hold and stroke her hand. Eventually she calmed down and the two began to reminisce about old times.

Mr. Newell, when explaining to Patricia the household and occupants, had told her Moran had joined the household as the duchess' personal secretary almost fifty years ago. She had funded his medical studies, after which he'd served as her private physician, residing at Pemberley House ever since.

Seeing now the way Moran held the duchess' hand and spoke to her, and their behavior together earlier in the hothouse, Patricia was sure he must have been her lover as well. She must have taken him when she was a middle-aged woman and he was young. He must be almost forty years her junior, but she was wealthy and he was entranced by her, apparently, although he must have had other women. But he must be perverted to be so fascinated by her and become her lover. Or perhaps it was just a matter of money. She was willing to buy a young lover. Now, he was 65 and she 103, a doctor and patient with lecherous memories to share.

Then Patricia thought of the age difference between her own parents, twenty-six years. Was twenty-six years really all that different from thirty-eight? Perhaps not. If it was, she was in no position to judge, she chided herself. After all, her own sexual fantasies about her father and displacing her mother in his eyes were, if not lecherous, psychologically deviant.

She hadn't appreciated the duchess' judgmental comments, and now here she was reciprocating, although she didn't give voice to her thoughts as the duchess had. Still, if the duchess and Moran had been happy, it was none of her business, she supposed, continuing to watch them. Although she had a hard time imagining the duchess as a happy woman.

Everyone had their hang-ups, and she resolved be more tolerant and give the inhabitants of Pemberley House another chance. Then she realized, snapping out of her internal monologue, that the duchess and Moran were returning her stare, and the old doctor asked if she was all right.

At the same time, she felt something on her thigh. It was Richard's right hand, wandering up under her dress.

"Quite all right, thank you Doctor. Still just a little tired from yesterday's…journey, I suppose." Patricia unobtrusively palmed her fork, slipped it under the white linen table cloth, and stabbed the tines down into the back of Richard's hand.

Richard emitted a brief yelp and the hand withdrew.

"What the devil is going on over there?"

"Nothing, duchess," Richard managed to get out, "just swallowed the wrong way. Not to worry, sorry."

Carla knew better, and smirked at her brother. She caught Patricia's eye and half-winked. Across but under the table, Carla slipped off her spiked heel and extended her leg, running her toes along Patricia's calf, up her inner thigh, and under her skirt. She grinned and licked her lips. Patricia allowed a small smile in return.

She didn't use the fork.

"Well, I've had enough of these shenanigans," the duchess said. "Augustus, take me up to bed, although I don't think I'll sleep a wink tonight."

"Of course, duchess," Moran replied and the two bade their good-nights to the others.

"I think I'll retire too," Patricia said.

"Come to the library for a cognac before bed?" Carla asked.

"Well, all right."

The library was one of the house's more masculine rooms. Carla told her it was decorated and organized much like the sixth duke had left it. Built-in wooden bookcases stood floor-to-ceiling on three sides of the room, displaying even rows of ancient and modern works. Big game rifles were displayed on the fourth wall and in cabinets. A sealed display case that also ran along the fourth wall contained various arcane objects, among them a harpoon with the initials "N.L." carved on the hilt (identified as part of the original Phileas Fogg Collection, c. 1866, on loan from the neighboring estate of Fogg Shaw in Derbyshire), and, most notably, several pieces of metal debris and fragments arranged in the shape of a partial axe-head, the label under which read, "Axe shards; provenance, Zu-Vendis, c. 1886."

Coats-of-armor, the real articles, marked by the dents and scratches of battle, flanked the stone frame and mantle of the library's huge fireplace. Club chairs in chocolate brown leather were arranged in front of the fire. The Kodiak bear rug on the floor before the fireplace reminded Patricia of the one on which she had seen her father and mother making love.

Patricia and Carla sat on a leather sofa near the high windows which let out onto the terrace. The rain continued to pound. Richard poured the drinks while Miss Neston stoked the fire and then took her leave.

Richard distributed the glasses and sat on the arm of the sofa next to Patricia. She got up and browsed a bookshelf dedicated to volumes of rare books of special interest to the sixth duke. Among them were Sherlock Holmes' *The Whole Art of Detection*, *Practical Handbook of Bee Culture, With Some Observations Upon the Segregation of the Queen,* and various other monographs and pamphlets by the Great Detective; Hendrik van Helsing's *Hollow Dark Places;* the two-volume in-quarto *Les Mystères des grands fonds sous-marins* (*Mysteries of the Great Submarine Depths*) by Professor Pierre Arronax; Ludvig Prinn's *De Vermis Mysteriis;* a charred copy of *How I Did It* by Victor von Frankenstein (Patricia pulled out a note tucked in the front of the volume; it indicated, in a woman's handwriting, that the book had been rescued from a burnt laboratory in the nearby village of Upper Fogg Shaw); Campion Bond's *Memoirs of an English Intelligencer, A Ghost in the Manor: A Romance* by Catherine Tilney; *The Ruthvenian;* and *Some Observations Upon a Series of Kalmuk Skulls* and *The Sahhindar Cult in Pre-Diluvian Khokarsa,* both by Professor George Edward Challenger.

Next she moved to a shelf set aside for books written by immediate family members, such as John Cecil Clayton's *An Odyssey in the American Wilderness* and Mary Bennet's *Selected Observations and Moral Extractions. Excessively Diverted, Or, Leaving Pemberley* looked intriguing; it was a thin, privately printed pamphlet by Delhi Darcy, and Patricia resolved to come back to it later. *The Dynamics of an Asteroid* and *A Treatise on the Binomial Theorem* by Professor James Moriarty appeared out of place, and Patricia assumed they were misfiled. She also wondered what Moriarty could possibly have added to the subject of the Binomial Theorem that was worth an entire treatise.

Prominently and, it seemed to her, more appropriately displayed were the works of General Sir William Clayton, Bt.: *Gold and a Lost Love in Africa, Blood and Love among the Redskins, Love Is a Jaguar,* and his masterpiece, the three volume autobiography *Never Say Die: The Memoirs of One Who Always Heard the Distant Trumpet.*

Richard approached behind her. "That last is extremely rare, coz, perhaps the only remaining copy. The sixth duke was mortified at his uncle's indelicacies, and put his considerable energies to suppressing it and destroying all known copies."

"Hmmm." Patricia walked away and stood at the window, staring at the downpour.

"You really should be nicer to me, you know," Richard said.

"Oh? Why is that," she asked without turning.

He came up and stood behind her again, tilting his head to speak into her ear. Carla watched. "Bess appears tonight," Richard said. "Are you sure you want to face her alone?"

"Quite sure. Besides, when you told me about it last night in the car, you laughed it off as a silly legend."

"Maybe it is. Maybe it isn't. Not being a direct descendent, like you, I'll never know." He bent closer to her ear and put a hand around her waist. "I think, my dear Patricia, you'd best take me up on my offer. I can protect you."

Patricia turned and faced him. At six feet tall without heels, she didn't need to look up at him. His hand was still on her waist. Carla still watched them, transfixed. "Mr. Deguy, all I need protection from, I think, is you."

"And all you need, Miss Wildman, I think, is a good fucking."

Patricia's knee slammed into Richard's crotch, followed by the heel of her hand smashing into his nose. He doubled over, writhing in pain and spilling his drink. Carla was breathing hard. A bead of sweat showed on her upper lip in the firelight. Her right hand moved under her skirt, while she sipped her drink with her left.

Patricia half-registered Carla's excitement, but she remained focused on Richard squirming on the floor. Blood and mucus poured from his nose and covered his face. She spoke to him. "Let me make it abundantly clear, Richard. In the twenty-four hours since I've arrived here, you've taunted me with stories about the ghost of Bess. You got a blowjob from a drunken barmaid in the front seat of the car while chauffeuring me from the train station."

Carla's eyes widened at this revelation, as Patricia went on.

"You ran off God knows where when those two waylaid us on the road. I had to free myself, and you have the balls to suggest you'll protect me. You were fucking the barmaid—who is obviously pregnant, probably by you—out in the woods today."

Richard began to stand up as Patricia continued to speak. "Maybe I do need a good fucking. Probably I do. But I guarantee that when and if I get that good fucking, it's not going to be from

you. And if it were you, there's no way in hell it would be good."
Patricia tossed the rest of her drink in his face and he yelled as the
alcohol burned his eyes.

"Goddamn, you little bitch, I'm—"

"You'll do nothing," Carla said. "Get out of here, Richard."

"But—"

"Out."

Richard cast a look of pure hatred at Patricia and left. The
door slammed in its ancient wooden frame.

Patricia continued to stand and Carla sat. They watched each
other, silently, as the rain drummed a beat against the windows.

Then Carla spoke. "Blowjob in the Rolls, huh?"

"Yeah."

"While he was driving, with you in the back?"

"Yeah."

Carla was quiet for a bit more. Then: "Slimeball deserved it."

"Yeah."

The two women burst out in laughter, and Carla poured more
cognac. "That was an excellent Rémy Martin you tossed all over
Richard and the floor."

"Sorry."

"Don't be." Carla handed Patricia her glass. "He had it coming. And you had me coming."

Patricia was embarrassed. "It turns you on to see your brother
getting the shit beat out of him?"

"You turn me on. Where did you learn to fight like that,
anyway?"

"My father. It's a long story."

"I have time."

"I really don't feel like talking about it tonight. I'm sorry,
Carla."

"That's all right."

Patricia downed the last of her drink. "In fact, I think it's time
to call it a night."

Carla gazed at her a long while, then shrugged. "At least let me
walk you back to your room."

Patricia nodded, and the two women walked without speaking through the dark, winding corridors and ornate passages to Patricia's room on the second floor. All was still in the house, the silence punctuated by the cracks of thunder as the storm outside continued to rage and roil.

They arrived at Patricia's door and stood there.

"Well, good night, then."

"Patricia, I hope I'm not as repulsively forward as my brother… In fact, I hope you don't find me in any way repulsive."

"No, of course not. I don't think you're anything like your brother."

"Invite me in, then?" Carla asked.

"Not tonight…"

"Have I misread you? You don't like girls?"

"I like…I've been with a girl, once. Twice. Mostly men. I was married, once. I only just met you," Patricia said. "Why am I telling you all this?"

"You like me."

Carla put one hand on Patricia's breast and grabbed her bottom with the other. She gently raised her left knee between Patricia's legs and began rubbing up and down. She circled Patricia's now hard nipple through the blouse's diaphanous fabric with her thumb. Carla put her hand behind Patricia's neck and pulled her mouth down to hers, darting and exploring with her tongue. Patricia reciprocated, pulling Carla hard against her, enjoying the feeling of Carla's full breasts against her own.

Carla felt up under Patricia's skirt and began to massage her, bringing on a wave of ecstasy. But when she slipped the wet panties aside and began to slip a finger inside, Patricia stopped her.

"What is it," Carla said.

"Just…I can't." Patricia was out of breath and felt a little dizzy. "I do like you, you're right. But not tonight."

Carla exhaled and tried to catch her breath. "All right, then. Good night, and sleep tight." She kissed Patricia once more, deeply. Then she collected herself and tiptoed off down the hall toward her own room.

Patricia watched her go, then fumbled with the doorknob to her own room. She felt disoriented. She must've had too much to drink, on top of all she'd been through in the past day. And the past few weeks.

She heard a noise.

From the end of the hall, opposite the direction Carla had just departed, Peter Parker stepped out of the shadows.

"You! How long have you been standing there, watching?" Patricia whispered. "Is everyone in this house a fucking pervert?"

"I came to warn you, Patricia. Be careful..."

"Of what?" she asked, still seething.

"I'm not sure. But things aren't right around here."

"I'll say. Well, thank you Pete, and good night." She got the door open and scampered in before he could say another word. She shut the door in his face and left him standing alone in the dark.

12.

PATRICIA LOCKED THE door, fuming.

She'd liked Parker. She had trusted him and found him attractive. Now it turned out he was a degenerate like the rest of them. Carla might be okay, but even she had shocked Patricia a bit when she had gotten excited over Patricia pummeling Richard.

Imagine—the groundskeeper, a Peeping Tom!

Patricia took a hot bath to relax. She drained the tub, put on a light negligee, and double-checked the locks on the hall door and the French windows.

Outside, the storm raged.

She closed the curtains and came to bed. There was a stack of magazines and books on the night table. The maid must have brought them, because they hadn't been there earlier in the afternoon.

She stoked the fire in the ancient grate to ward off the chill and flipped through the pile of magazines and slim volumes.

The New Adventures of Fanny Hill, or, The Further Adventures of a Woman of Pleasure, as recounted to Mr. John Cleland; the Marquis de Sade's *Justine, or, Good Conduct Well Chastised*; Swinburne's *Lesbia Brandon* and *Poetica Erotica*; a copy of *The Saxon Blake Library*; an English translation of Camillo Boito's *Senso*; *As You Desire* by William Norfolk, M.D.; *Lady Chatterley's Lover* by D.H. Lawrence;

Doyle's *The Return of Sherlock Holmes*; and *Love of War and Women*, a volume of Victorian erotic poetry by Sir William Clayton.

The maid—or whoever assembled the collection of reading materials for her—seemed to be as obsessed with sex as everyone else in Pemberley House. Or maybe someone was trying to send her a message.

Patricia flipped open the book of Holmes stories and saw it had been bookmarked at "The Adventure of the Priory School." Then she changed her mind and selected the book of Swinburne poetry. She turned down the lights, leaving the candle on the nightstand burning, and climbed in bed. She opened the book at random to "Love and Sleep."

That seems promising, two things I need a lot of right now, she thought, and read on.

> Lying asleep between the strokes of night
> I saw my love lean over my sad bed,
> Pale as the duskiest lily's leaf or head,
> Smooth-skinned and dark, with bare throat made to bite,
> Too wan for blushing and too warm for white,
> But perfect-coloured without white or red.
> And her lips opened amorously, and said—
> I wist not what, saving one word—Delight.
>
> And all her face was honey to my mouth,
> And all her body pasture to mine eyes;
> The long lithe arms and hotter hands than fire
> The quivering flanks, hair smelling of the south,
> The bright light feet, the splendid supple thighs
> And glittering eyelids of my soul's desire.

Or, maybe not, she thought.

She still felt a little lightheaded, and told herself she was mentally and physically exhausted. Sleep would cure what ailed her, but sleep wouldn't come. She tried to focus on the Swinburne, but was distracted by the surroundings in her chamber. The lascivious paintings of satyrs and nymphs by Caravaggio, the Old Italian master, seemed to dance and whirl in the flickering candlelight. She forced her eyes back down to the book resting on her breasts, and the words also danced on the page, rendering them illegible.

It continued to storm, and Patricia remembered Richard telling her tempests were a tradition on the anniversary of Bess's murder by her fourth husband. Well, strictly speaking, the anniversary was tomorrow night, but that was a technicality; Bess was to appear three nights running and this was the first night.

Could occult legends have technicalities? Did they follow strict, immutable laws, or was there room to maneuver? Must Bess appear tonight? And only here at Pemberley, only to a descendent of the d'Arcys? Was Bess locked into a preordained set of actions and reactions?

Or did spirits have free will?

Could a ghost break the rules, if she really wanted to?

Patricia felt like she was floating, and a disconnected part of her brain railed at the other part for spending precious mental resources deconstructing ghosts and goblins. Her father would not have bought that nonsense. He would have found a rational explanation for it.

For what, the other part of her brain asked sardonically? Nothing's happened. Yet.

And nothing will, the rational side replied.

She finally drifted off, continuing to dream and debate with herself.

13.

THUNDER RUMBLED AND Patricia awoke with a start, her heart pounding in her throat. The wind blew open the French windows with a crash, although she was sure she had secured them. Lightning ripped open the sky again and white light flashed in her room, causing the satyrs and devils to leap off the canvas. Wind whipped at the drapes and swung the window back and forth as hard rain splashed in.

Patricia jumped out of bed, which was raised on a foot-high dais, and bent over to pull on her slippers. She tottered and grabbed a bedpost to support her. The bedpost wriggled and squirmed in her hand. She jerked away with a shudder. She still felt somewhat unsettled, although not as much as when she had gone to sleep.

She went to the windows and began to close them against the storm when she saw dark shapes moving around on the grounds outside. It was hard to make them out in the downpour, but there were definitely two people outside in the torrent.

What the hell could they be doing?

She thought about calling the police, and then hesitated. What if it's Richard and his lover meeting again? she thought. While she found his behavior disgusting, she wasn't the moral police and had no desire to get involved.

She looked at the clock; it was 11:55, and she remembered Bess's ghost was supposed to appear at 12 midnight. Then she realized she wasn't thinking clearly. Even if it was Richard, he wasn't engaging in a lover's tryst outside in the midst of a raging lightning storm. It was Richard, however, who continually reminded her about the Pemberley Curse, even as he downplayed it as a silly fairy tale or a joke. With midnight approaching, Richard and someone else must be outside, perhaps getting ready to play a joke on her, or something even more serious.

The carved bedposts of Bess of Pemberley's bed looked as if they were crawling and slithering with half-man, half-beast things as lightning continued to split the darkness, and the salacious paintings and scenes of naked people being tortured were full of life and evil. She wondered if she were dreaming. Or perhaps something from dinner was making her ill. She began to get a bit frightened.

Maybe she should get Parker, and see if he could help her find out what was going on. Perhaps he had meant well and she had been hasty in running him off.

Patricia decided not to call the police; she wanted to spoil Richard's little joke—if it was Richard, and if it was a joke. She decided she'd investigate herself. She didn't want to alert the intruders outside that they'd been seen, so she kept the lights off in her room. She fumbled around the unfamiliar room in the dark and, navigating by the occasional flashes of lightning, was able to locate her robe. Standing in front of Bess's gilt-edged mirror, she tied the satin garment around her waist. The wind gusted in the still-open French windows, flipping up the robe and exposing her, which she could see by lightning in the mirror. She ran over and secured the windows against the elements, and then sat on the foot of the bed, facing the mirror again, watching herself pull on her slippers.

She stood, and lightning flashed again. The clock struck midnight and she saw in the mirror, or thought she saw, standing behind her and over her shoulder, a reflection of a woman's pale figure.

Carla!

The woman was wearing a white shift and her dark hair was styled differently, but beyond that it was undoubtedly Carla.

Patricia whirled, terrified. "What are you doing in here? How did you get in—" Patricia broke off. The woman was gone.

Was her mind playing tricks?

She ran to the hall door, opened it, and looked both ways. No one was there. She went down the stairs and to the main hall, picked the first door on her right, and entered the study. She dashed through the room and yanked on the garden windows which opened onto the house's huge portico, heedless of the storm. She was determined to give Richard hell. Any ruckus could cause the old woman to die of shock, and this was two nights in a row now, although they had all determined not to tell her about the prior evening's goings-on. Still, the old duchess had already been worked up about Bess's supposed appearance tonight, and although Patricia was not very fond of the ancient, lecherous, acid-tongued bitch, she didn't want her to die prematurely either.

Well, Patricia corrected herself, going off to the great beyond at the ripe old age of 103 might not exactly be accurately characterized as premature, but she didn't want a needless and senseless shock to send her off before her time, whenever that might be.

One of the people she had seen outside her window might have been Richard, but his companion couldn't have been Carla, since Carla was otherwise occupied skulking around Patricia's room. But how did Carla get in and out so fast, and without Patricia seeing her? Were the siblings both trying to scare her, or was Richard acting on his own in that regard? Carla had another motive for coming to Patricia's room in the dead of night, even if they had earlier said their good-nights. But why had Carla disappeared when Patricia confronted her?

She crept further down the veranda and saw the two figures approach the house. She ducked down close to the carved stone balustrade so they wouldn't see her in a random lightning flash, and continued to crawl forward. The rain plastered her thin robe to her body and she shivered.

Patricia was now close enough to see the two prowlers. Neither of them was Richard. For that matter, neither of them was Carla, though she had expected that, since Carla's main business seemed to be creeping about Patricia's room uninvited.

The two intruders were Jack Hare and the woman Ernie. They looked the worse for wear, with black eyes and bruises about their faces where Patricia had beaten them with the wooden stakes the previous night.

They forced open a window and entered the house. Patricia had to give the alarm now. She saw red and wanted to go after them herself. After all, she had every reason to hate them for assaulting her, and she had driven them off on her own last night.

But she still felt unwell from the food poisoning at dinner—at least she thought it must be food poisoning that had made her so disoriented and dizzy—and decided it was better to confront the trespassers with strength in numbers.

She ran back down the length of the porch and reentered the house at the study where she had exited, a few rooms down from the room into which Ernie and Jack had gone. She found a house phone and rang through to Parker. After she explained the situation, she went back outside to meet him.

A few minutes later, she saw the beam of a flashlight and called out to Parker, who joined her on the terrace near the window the two crooks had entered. He carried a rifle.

"I thought you weren't speaking to me," he said.

"I wasn't, but this took precedence."

"Okay, you're sure it's the two who grabbed you last night?"

"Yes. At first I thought it might be Richard and someone else, maybe Carla. But Carla showed up in my room—"

"Where is she now?"

"No idea, she disappeared. Anyway, I caught a close look as they broke in. It's definitely Ernie and Jack."

"All right, I'll go in and find them. You get inside too, you're drenched and practically naked, and it's freezing out here."

Patricia raised her eyebrow. "I'm not surprised you noticed the naked part, Pete."

"Well, it's hard to miss. That robe is so plastered to your skin it might as well be invisible." He looked her up and down, pausing at her full breasts. "And you are clearly chilled to the bone. But I wasn't spying on your—your embrace earlier tonight. I really did come to warn you. I hope you believe me. But we don't have time for this, we can sort it out later."

She nodded. "All right."

"I'm going in now, here. I think you should go back inside at a different part of the house and call the police." He raised a hand in mock salute and started to climb in the window.

Before he could take another step, the glass in the French doors the next room over burst outward, followed by a naked man tumbling out the window, up and over the low stone railing around the veranda, and down onto the vast lawn.

The man was short and scrawny, covered in patches of black matted hair. It was Austin, the chauffer. He ran away from the house in a limping zig-zag pattern which looked designed to evade gunfire.

It was.

A barrage of bullets blazed orange from the window Austin had crashed through, followed by the pistols and their wielders, Jack and Ernie. The two black-clad interlopers hopped over the terrace and onto the lawn in pursuit of Austin, still firing.

The breaking glass and gunfire raised alarms and security lights began to come on around the house and grounds. Parker knelt on the portico and used the granite balustrade to steady his aim at the fleeing figures. He got off several shots at Ernie and Jack and they scattered. Austin, meanwhile, scampered up a tree like the small monkey he resembled.

The shots continued and then let up. After a few minutes without shooting, Patricia saw Austin scurry down out of the tree and dash back to the house. He climbed back up the veranda, and made for the inside.

"Hold on there, then," Parker said. He grabbed Austin's arm.

"Sod off, Parker," Austin said, "'less you want a bloody stump where that hand is now." He yanked his arm back and kept on walking.

Patricia gawked, wide-eyed, at Austin. His flaccid member was almost as big as her father's, although that seemed impossible. She tried to banish thoughts of her father and told Parker, "Careful, Pete, he might actually have a blade concealed somewhere under that pelt."

"Shut it, girlie," Austin tossed back as he rounded a corner and disappeared up the stairs.

"Ex-con...and the Duchess likes him, huh?" Patricia said. Parker shrugged.

"What about Ernie and Jack?" she asked.

"What about them?" a new voice demanded.

Patricia and Parker turned to find old Doctor Moran in the doorway, disheveled in his nightclothes. He held some sort of odd-looking cane and was surveying them and the damage to the French windows. A woman in a mousy nightdress cowered behind him and peeked over his shoulder.

Patricia started, shocked. Was that the duchess? They couldn't have actually been having sex. Could they? It was unthinkable, at her age. Then the woman moved a bit to the side and Patricia saw it was the housekeeper, Mrs. Abingdon. It was clear they were both surprised in bed.

So the old doctor is a horny bastard, she thought.

"What about Ernie and Jack?" the old man repeated. "What the hell is going on here?"

While Patricia and Parker explained, Richard and Carla joined the party. Like Patricia and Parker, they were soaked through from the storm. Patricia noticed that Carla's dark nipples showed through the thin cotton blouse, hard from the cold and rain. She looked away, and tried with difficulty to refocus her attention on the discussion.

"Well then, where are this Ernie and Jack?" Richard was asking.

"They got away," Parker said.

"Well done, Pete, well done. A fine shot you must be," Richard drawled.

"And just what were you and Carla up to out there, then?"

"None of your damn business. Mind your place, Pete."

"It's a valid question," Patricia said.

"And I say it's no concern of yours, you bi—"

Carla had Richard's wrist in her hand and squeezed it hard. "Richard, lay off. It's a valid question. Richard saw something, or people, out and about in the storm, just like you did, Patricia. He came to get me and we investigated."

Parker looked doubtful, but before he could respond, Austin hobbled back downstairs, his fur-covered body now wrapped in a pale blue terrycloth bathrobe. He was followed by Jenkins, a gardener who lived off the estate, also in a state of undress.

"Bloody hell," Richard said. "What's he doing here?"

"Pretty obvious," Carla said.

"What of it?" Austin was a belligerent bulldog.

"Nothing of it," Carla said. "What did Jack Hare and Ernie want with you?"

"Who the hell're Jack Hare and—"

"The two who broke in here after you?" Parker said. "You remember? Breaking glass? Gunshots? Scurrying up the tree out there like a gibbon?"

"All right, all right. Just didn't know their names, is all."

"So," Patricia said, "why are they after you?"

"They are not—fucking—after me. Got it? They broke in, I heard 'em, came out of me room, they started shooting. That's it."

"Very well, then," Moran said. "Have the police been called?"

"I was about to," Patricia said, "but it happened so fast I didn't have a chance."

"Good. Parker, I trust you'll see to the repairs here and put some of your men on guard duty until morning."

Parker nodded once.

"Then everyone back to bed."

"Shouldn't we still call the police?" Patricia asked.

"No." Richard was vehement. "And not a word of this to the duchess," he added. He looked particularly at Patricia and Parker. "We don't want her becoming too excited, right?"

"Of course not," Patricia said.

"Then good night to you." Richard turned on his heel and marched off. "Coming, sis?" he called.

Carla looked after her brother's receding form, gave Patricia a quick kiss on the cheek, and followed him. Everyone else was already dispersing. Parker was busy speaking with the gardener, Jenkins.

She stole away to her room, turned on all the lights, and locked the door. Then she double-checked and secured the French doors.

The illness, the lightheadedness, she had felt earlier in the evening had passed. The salacious paintings and tapestries hung innocently. The carved bedposts didn't writhe, although the eye of a serpent wrapped around one of the posts seemed to stare at her. If serpents had eyebrows, this one would have raised his questioningly at her.

She sat down on the edge of the bed and peered into the mirror. Carla, or not-Carla, did not appear in the reflection over her shoulder. Could it have been Carla she saw in her room? These old houses were full of secret passages.

But how could it have been Carla, if she had been outside with Richard?

Or had it really been Bess d'Arcy, beholden by the Pemberley Curse to come haunt Patricia?

14.

T HE NEXT DAY, the mood was strained in Pemberley
House. Breakfast was served late due to the prior
evening's events, and the air was thick with tension,
especially at the sexual discoveries: old Doctor Moran and Mrs.
Abingdon, and Austin in bed with another man. All were still
concerned not to tell the duchess anything. The old lady took
breakfast in her room this morning.

Patricia suspected there was much more to last night's tumult.
Ernie and Jack could have just happened to enter the house near
Austin's quarters, but why were they trying to get into the house?
She thought about the late-night carjacking in the middle of an
uproarious storm. And what was it Jack had said that night? Jack
couldn't find him, and Ernie had replied that it wasn't him, he
wasn't driving.

Who did Ernie mean by "he"? Certainly not Richard, because
Richard was the driver. Richard had told Patricia that Austin was
down with a lame leg after being attacked by poachers and so
Austin hadn't been driving that night. Then the night prior Ernie
and Jack just happened to break in the house near Austin's quarters
and come after him.

Patricia was a genius, taking after her father, a man one of
New York's biggest newspapers had once called "a combination of

Leonardo da Vinci, Sherlock Holmes, Croesus, and Tarzan." But it didn't take a genius to see Jack and Ernie were the supposed poachers and they were after the chauffer, Austin, for some reason.

What wasn't clear was why no one else had come to the same conclusion. Or else, they had, but had their own reasons for not pursuing it.

Richard was up to something, it was obvious, and it was beginning to look like Carla was part of it. Richard's bluster with Parker last night was intended to deflect any more questions about whatever they had been up to out in the howling storm. Carla played the good cop, but her story about also investigating outside didn't ring true. In addition to a genius-level IQ and distinctive bronze-colored skin, Patricia also inherited near super-human eyesight from her father, and those curious, golden-flecked eyes surely would have seen anyone else in the night, especially when the lightning unpeeled the darkness.

Richard and Carla had been out in the torrent, to be sure, but not on the side of the house outside Patricia's room where she had seen Ernie and Jack skulking around.

Which meant they were lying, as well. What dirty secrets were they hiding?

It seemed everyone at Pemberley had them, the dirty secrets. The duchess did, even if they lingered from a moldering and decadent age; everyone who cared about her secrets must be long dead. Old horny Doctor Moran and his conquests. Richard and Carla. The chauffer.

What about Parker, did he have them too?

She was so disgusted she was almost ready to quit and leave, but still, she could clear out the whole place when she was baroness.

The denizens of Pemberley had all been up much of the night before, and so after breakfast everyone went their own way. Patricia avoided everyone. She spent the rest of the day alone and took the remainder of her meals by herself in her chamber.

She opened the curtains and pulled open the French windows for fresh air. The moist chill of early spring hung in the atmosphere, but was invigorating. For the time being the sky was clear, though black clouds roiled on the horizon. She picked a volume at random out of the reading pile and pulled a chair onto the terrace outside her windows.

In her hands was the Sherlock Holmes book. Holmes had been one of her father's greatest instructors and she was intrigued. She opened the book to the marked story, "The Adventure of the Priory School." Someone obviously wanted her to read it, so she would.

The tale was a quick but engaging read, and when she finished it, she realized how it related to her conversation yesterday with the duchess. The old lady had told her the Great Detective had come many years ago to investigate the kidnapping of her son, Arthur. "Priory School" told that tale, although Doctor Watson, or his editor, Doyle, had altered a few of the names for publication. He changed the name of the duke's illegitimate son, James Clarke Wildman, to "James Wilder." Pemberley House became "Holdernesse Hall," while the sixth Duke of Greystoke became the sixth Duke of Holdernesse. The nearby village of Lambton was called "Chesterfield," and the duchess was called "Edith Appledore" rather than her true name Edith Jansenius. Patricia knew from Mr. Newell that the full name of the James Wildman's half-brother Arthur, the seventh duke, was William Cecil Arthur Clayton. Other than the name changes, Watson's recitation of the case seemed to adhere to the duchess' version of the story in all particulars.

Now in a mood for detective stories, Patricia grabbed the magazine entitled *The Saxon Blake Library*. The painted cover showed a youngish man with a round face and fair hair confronting two other men with a gun. One of the other men was lean and hawk-faced with black hair slicked back from his forehead and cut with a neat part. He was dressed elegantly in a dark suit, overcoat, and spats. He held a homburg in his hands and somewhat resembled pictures she had seen of Sherlock Holmes. The other man was younger with a tweed coat and cap. The top corner of the magazine was emblazoned with, "The Leading Detective Magazine, New Series, No. 125." Across the bottom ran the title of the lead story.

"The Shades of Pemberley."

Below the title was a small caption: "A baffling tale of haunting by a 350-year-old spirit. Can Blake and Topper's first-rate detective work lay the ghost to rest before she comes again?"

Patricia was amazed. She gingerly opened the cover and looked at the date: January 1928. How could this be? How could there be a story about the Pemberley ghost in a forty-year-old pulp magazine?

She turned to the beginning of the tale and began to read.

"The Shades of Pemberley"
by Anon.

"Mr. Blake, I come on a matter of some delicacy..."
[Patricia read]

"I assure you, you may speak freely in front of my apprentice and confidant, Mr. Topper, with the same confidence in his discretion that you may have in mine. Likewise, your patroness has the same guarantee."

"That's very good of you, Mr. Blake, Mr. Topper." Augustus Moran, a young, fair-haired man of perhaps nineteen or twenty, was visibly relieved. "For I fear the Dowager Duchess of Holdernesse may be going mad!"

Moran.

Then, just as in the Holmes tale, Holdernesse was being used as an alternate or code-name for Greystoke. She read on.

J. Saxon Blake was a crack investigator who had studied with and worked alongside some of the best in Europe, including Sherlock Holmes, Nelson Lee, Sir Eric Palmer, and Erast Fandorin. He was also an expert in chemistry, rare poisons, fingerprints, strange cults, inks, firearms, and cryptography. Unlike Holmes, his cases occasionally veered into the realm of the fantastic, though not often. Topper, his assistant, was a brave, curly-haired lad full of intelligence and energy.

Blake and Topper had been in their consulting room when the caller had arrived. The sleuth and his apprentice had had offices on Upper Baker Street since before Blake's friend and rival Holmes had retired to Sussex several years earlier. They had been perusing the *Globe* and smoking, when their housekeeper Mrs. Bardell knocked, entered, and presented their visitor's card.

"Hum, hmmm. Remarkable." The detective carelessly tossed the card on the settee. Striding over to the bay window, he pulled aside the curtains and peered down through the heavy fog. The newly installed electric lamps barely cut through the miasma of the infernal pea soup, but he observed a 1925 Rolls Royce Phantom Sedanca De Ville motor-car idling at the curb in front of their Baker Street digs. The Phantom appeared to be even more luxurious than Blake's own Grey Panther Rolls. "Very interesting."

"What, guv'nor?" cried Topper earnestly.

"Ahem," the long-suffering Mrs. Bardell interpolated.

"Hmm? Oh, yes! By all means, Mrs. Bardell, by all means, show him up."

Blake paced with the lean, nervous energy that still propelled him in early middle-age, his grey eyes alight with excitement, as two sets of footsteps proceeded up the familiar steps, until finally the landlady entered with their caller.

Blake sprang past the davenport, his favorite pipe clenched firmly between his teeth, and greeted their guest with a firm, dry handshake. "Come in, Mr. Moran. Please, sit here by the fire and warm yourself. Cigarette? This is my associate, Topper—Topper, pull that extra armchair over here, good man. Mr. Moran, what brings you from Derbyshire to London this brumous morning?"

Now all three men were ensconced before the warming grate. Mrs. Bardell had served coffee and whisky, and Mr. Moran's discretionary concerns had been allayed.

"The Duchess of Holdernesse—going mad?" Blake fired his pipe and sat back, drawing his dressing gown up around him. "Pray continue," he murmured.

"Very well," their guest said. "I assume you deduced my connection to the duchess from my card?"

Blake waved him on, impatiently. "Yes, you currently reside at Pemberley House, and the duchess is well known as the holder of that venerable estate. What role do you play in the household, sir?"

It seemed that Moran reddened slightly, but he responded that he was currently pursuing a medical education. "I am at present the duchess' secretary. Our arrangement is that she will provide for my medical studies, and in turn I will serve as her personal physician once they are concluded."

"I see. Very convenient. Well, shall we proceed to the crux of the matter? Her madness?"

Moran took a deep breath. "Certainly. It has to do with the so-called 'Pemberley Curse.' Her Grace insists she's been haunted for the past several years by the ghost of her distant ancestor, Bess of Pemberley, on the anniversary of Bess's death. And the anniversary is three days hence."

"Fascinating," said Blake. "Did she send you here to engage my services, or are you here of your own accord?"

"The duchess sent me."

"And do you know the whole story of the curse?"

"I know the legend, yes. But surely you don't mean to place any credence in such nonsense?"

"Since the curse, real or not, is the underlying motivation for her proposal to secure my employment, I would posit that it is a valid starting place for our inquiry," Blake said pointedly. "If you please?"

"Very well. The Dowager Duchess," Moran began, clearly reluctant, "was married to the 6th Duke of Holdernesse. Pemberley House is an ancient estate located in the Midlands county of Derbyshire. The legend goes that the ghost of the murdered Baroness of Lambton, Bess d'Arcy, appears on the anniversary of her death to family members in her direct line of descent, but only on the premises of Pemberley House itself. The ghost appears at 12 o'clock midnight for three nights running: the night before the anniversary, the night of the anniversary, and the night after the anniversary. The legend has it if the ghost is shown love, not terror, she will go away forever."

"I see. And how did the curse come about?"

"This is most distasteful."

Blake arched an eyebrow at him.

"All right," Moran sighed. "Bess d'Arcy was a much-married Elizabethan woman who founded three houses, although she was not of the nobility herself. Her fourth husband was William d'Arcy, the Baron of Lambton. He was an immensely wealthy landowner, and the holder of Pemberley House in the late 16th century. William and Bess had two children, Christopher and Jane d'Arcy.

"The triggering event was Bess d'Arcy's infidelity with Captain Philip Fermier, in 1569. William d'Arcy put Bess's lover Fermier to death, and later murdered his wife on the day of Jane's birth in 1570."

"So the curse began then?" Blake interrupted.

"No, the supposed curse was placed on the family in 1592, on Jane d'Arcy's 22nd birthday. The occasion was a grand feast in honor of Jane's birthday and engagement to Captain John Caldwell-Grebson.

"Caldwell-Grebson had heard tales of the hospitality of Pemberley House years ago from the late Captain Philip Fermier, who obviously never returned from his final visit to the estate. The wealthy Caldwell-Grebson had concluded long years of privateering and had stopped at the Pemberley estate on his way to his ancestral home. He extended his stay at Pemberley House when he became enamored with Jane d'Arcy, and they were quickly affianced.

"Jane had had what could be generously called an unhappy childhood—"

"Little wonder, with a father who murdered her mother!" exclaimed Topper.

"Well, Mr. Topper, William never believed he was Jane's father, and treated her accordingly. The engagement to Captain Caldwell-Grebson was probably the first happiness the girl had known.

"The feast, the story goes, was a grand affair, with guests in attendance from all over England and even beyond. Legend has it that one of these was a necromancer who was also a relative of the late Fermier. This is where the story becomes truly ridiculous," Moran trailed off.

Blake gestured for him to proceed, and their guest did so, with another sigh. "Of course, no one knew any of this as the festivities began, but the occultist quickly made himself known, and laid a curse on the family as vengeance for Fermier's death years before. The curse, as I have said, is that Bess would appear to her direct descendants, and her murderer of course, in Pemberley House, on the anniversary of her murder.

"The spell was conditional, in effect giving William a chance to avoid it, or else hoist himself by his own petard. If Jane d'Arcy was really the legitimate daughter of William, then the curse would take effect and be passed on to all subsequent generations of d'Arcys. In that case, William could avoid passing on the curse by showing Bess's ghost love and repentance, rather than hatred and more violence. On the other hand, if Jane was really the illegitimate daughter of Fermier, then there would be no curse at all on the d'Arcys."

"What happened, sir?" asked Topper, engrossed by the tale.

"William d'Arcy, a cruel man by all accounts, was driven mad, and saw Bess everywhere, eventually mistaking his daughter for her. D'Arcy got his come-uppance, ending up in the madhouse, although not before murdering Jane, thinking in his madness that he was slitting Bess's throat once more, for that's how he had killed Bess twenty-two years prior.

"The upshot, or at least the legend, is the Pemberley Curse was indeed enacted; Jane was the daughter of William d'Arcy, not the illegitimate daughter of Fermier. And the curse was passed on to the children of Jane's older brother, Christopher d'Arcy, and their descendants."

"Awful!" Topper declared.

"Yes, indeed," agreed Moran. Blake made note of Moran's slight rolling of the eyes and the touch of a sarcastic tone, though the eager Topper seemed to miss it. "Anyway, Bess allegedly has been appearing to the d'Arcys and their descendants, off and on, for centuries. The dowager's father, Sir Charles Appledore, was a distant descendant. One of Christopher's daughters married a Hungarian count in the 1600s. The duchess' grandfather was originally from Hungary.

"Ironically, the d'Arcy and the Caldwell-Grebson families finally did come together years later when

Ursula d'Arcy married Ralph Arthur Caldwell-Grebson in 1667. So, as it happens, the duchess' late husband, the 6th Duke, was also a distant descendant of Christopher d'Arcy through the Caldwell-Grebsons. He passed away in '09.

"In any event, the story goes the ghost doesn't appear consistently—she seems to appear for a year or several years running, and then won't be seen for decades at a time. Indeed, it's only within the last few years that Her Grace has been afflicted.

"It's all twaddle, of course, but you asked," Moran concluded.

"I did, and it's very interesting twaddle indeed!" replied Blake, with characteristic good humor. "Tell me, Moran, since you choose not to believe the duchess, what you envision for my participation in this affair?"

"Why, show her the folly of it, of course!"

"Aha! And if it is not folly?"

"It is either folly, or she is mad."

"And madness wouldn't do, would it? Put you in a bit of a bad spot, I'd say."

"Gentlemen, I'll not sit here and be insulted like this." Moran stood. "Her Grace expects you at Pemberley House tomorrow morning. I trust I may convey that her expectations shall be satisfied?"

"Indeed, we wouldn't dare disappoint—Her Grace, that is."

Augustus Moran nodded once at each of them curtly, and showed himself out.

"Guv', was it wise to be so rude?" Topper exclaimed.

The sleuth chuckled. He had obviously conceived a strong dislike for Moran. "Just stirring things up, old son, see what shakes out. Here, hand me the telephone, would you, there's a good lad."

Blake spent a few minutes with the operator before being connected. Then: "Hallo? Hallo? Russell, is that you? It's Saxon Blake. Blake! Yes. Put Holmes on, would you?"

Another pause. "Hello, Holmes, it's Blake. Up in London, right now, yes. Sorry to tear you away from the beekeeping—it's keeping you well preserved, I trust? Fine, fine. Listen, Holmes, Topper and I received a rather odd visitor today, name of Augustus Moran. You don't think—? His grandson? Yes, I thought as much. Says he came at the behest of Edith, Duchess of Holdernesse, up at Pemberley House. Yes, the very same, the Priory School case. The 6th Duke? Passed away almost twenty years ago, Moran said. The boy from the Priory School case must be the 7th Duke now. No? Of course! Thanks for reminding me. What? Says she's being haunted. Haunted, I said! Yes, yes, I know, 'no ghosts need apply' and all that. Well—Yes! Well, Holmes, must ring off now, need to prepare for the trip to Derbyshire. Yes, give my best to Russell, and kiss your niece Violet when you see her. Cute as button, I say. Goodbye now."

Blake hung up the telephone and grinned at his faithful apprentice. "'No ghosts need apply,' indeed!"

"Well guv', Mr. Holmes may have something, at that," Topper ventured.

"Oh, I know. Not our usual type of case, and normally I'd send it on to Carnacki or that American fellow, Dickson, who's set up shop down the street in Holmes' old digs. But this one is special. I took a case for the 6th Duke back in '04, a postscript of sorts to Holmes' work on the Priory School case. The Duke wanted to track down his illegitimate son, James Wildman, and didn't want Holmes to know about it, so he hired me."

"What happened, guv'nor?"

"The boy did quite well for himself. Had changed his name, had a son, and made his fortune. When

I found him, he was in pre-medical school at Johns Hopkins. Quite a success story!"

Blake returned to the present. "Anyway, we're keeping the case. So c'mon, young 'un, 'the game is afoot,' or something like that!"

Patricia's eyes began to droop. The events of the last few days, and indeed the last weeks and months, were still wearing on her.

The sun dipped over the horizon and a chill wind stirred up as the storm clouds rolled in.

She carried the chair back into her room and closed the windows. Large drops of rain began to pelt against the ancient leaded glass. She rang for dinner to be brought to her room, freshened up a bit in the washroom, and ate the soup and beef which had been delivered at her summons.

The Saxon Blake story was fascinating and seemed to align in almost every detail with the story of Bess which Richard had told her the night of her arrival. A few names were changed to protect the innocent—or more likely, the guilty. But the particulars seemed remarkably accurate. Her own grandfather, James Wildman, was mentioned in the tale under his own name.

Patricia also got a thrill out of Blake's mention of Holmes' niece. Violet Holmes had been her mother's best friend and a frequent visitor at the Wildmans' upstate New York residence. Patricia had stayed in touch with Violet after her parents' deaths, and couldn't wait to ring her up with the news that she was immortalized in the musty pages of the old magazine. She resolved to call her as soon as her legal business here at Pemberley was concluded.

Patricia stacked her dishes and tray on a side table, got undressed, and jumped into bed naked. She pulled the thick down duvet up over her breasts and tucked it in under her arms, then picked up the Blake magazine and continued reading.

Blake and Topper were bundled up in the back seat of the Phantom Sedanca De Ville, traveling down the Lambton high road. The village of Lambton, where the morning train had deposited the detective and his loyal assistant, was five miles from Pemberley House. The sun shown brilliantly today, although the chill of early spring still hung in the Derbyshire air.

"The Fighting Cock," noted Blake, as they passed an inn on their right.

"Then the Priory School...?" queried Topper.

"About six miles to the south"—Blake gestured to their left—"across the Lower Gill Moor. One of Holmes' greatest triumphs. Located the kidnapped son of the 6th Duke—not James Wildman, whom I mentioned to you earlier—and ran a murderous villain to ground. The scoundrel was Hayes, proprietor of the Fighting Cock, which we just passed. Don't recall the particulars, though. Ah, here we are, then."

The two men were quieted as a vast estate loomed through huge oak trees. They entered through a low road and drove a considerable distance through a beautiful wood. Finally as they ascended, there stood revealed the great house itself, a large, stately stone building set against further woody, rolling hills. The original manor house, framed by naturalistic gardens, had first been built in the mid-1500s, with various additions over the centuries. Mary's Tower, high on the hill behind Pemberley House, dated from the early 1580s. It was reputed that Mary, Queen of Scots, spent much time there.

Blake and Topper were shown in and escorted through a vast entrance hall, and down the Great Hall lined with massive portraits. One was of the late 6th Duke, a tall man with a curved nose, red beard, and grey eyes.

Topper tugged on Blake's sleeve and pointed to two other handsome portraits, whispering, "Look, guv', it's Darcy and Elizabeth!" referring to Fitzwilliam Darcy and his wife, Elizabeth Bennet, whose great courtship and love affair were made famous in Jane Austen's semi-biographical novel.

Finally they were shown into the dowager's sitting room, a tropical hothouse at one end of the building. The duchess, although she was now approaching 60 years of age, still displayed remnants of her youthful beauty, dark-eyed, delicately aquiline-nosed, with marked black eyebrows and straight mouth over a little chin. Her features showed a strong personality.

Moran made introductions, and the four sat down to discuss the business at hand.

"Well, Mr. Blake, my secretary has provided the particulars. Have you any thoughts on the matter?" the duchess began imperiously.

"In fact, Your Grace, I do," the sleuth replied. "But first, a few more questions. The ghost of Bess has not yet afflicted you this year?"

"No, the anniversary is two nights hence."

"And how many years has Bess appeared to you?"

"This would be the fourth."

"I see. Prior to the recent visitations, when was the ghost last seen at Pemberley House?"

"My late husband told me stories that his uncle, Sir William Clayton, was similarly afflicted when he stayed over in Pemberley one night. Sir William claimed to have given the ghost what it wanted, and that it would trouble the family no more. My husband refused to tell me exactly what it was Sir William had done. In any case, the Duke treated the whole story as a joke, as Sir William was well-known for his unreliability and instability."

"Sir William was also a renowned lover of life, as it were. You'll excuse my indelicacy, duchess, but he was famous, or infamous, as a lover of many women the world over, is that not the case?"

"Mr. Blake!" exclaimed Moran.

"Guv'nor, my stars!" came the cry from young Topper.

"Mr. Blake, I fail to see how such an impertinent question can be in any way related to the matter in question," the dowager replied. The temperature in the room dropped a few degrees.

"Yes, hmm, yes, I thought that might be the case," mumbled the detective to himself, lost in his thoughts, almost as if he was alone in the room.

"Mr. Blake!" the duchess interjected. "If we may have your attention? Kindly explain how you propose to address my problem, or else absent yourself from the premises and I will seek aid elsewhere!"

"My apologies, Your Grace, my apologies. It's all very clear to me."

"If you'd care to enlighten the rest of us…?"

"Yes, guv'," cried Topper, "tell us what we must do!"

"Not 'we,' Topper. Very well. Mr. Moran tells me the legend has it the ghost must be shown love, not fear. Correct?"

"That is the legend, yes, and it is nonsense," replied Moran.

"Well," Blake spoke to the duchess, ignoring Moran, "have you done so?"

"What are you implying? Certainly not!"

"You obviously accept the rest of the legend with your claim to be haunted by the ghost of Bess of Pemberley. Why do you reject this portion of the tale?" Blake inquired, coolly.

"You're mad."

"Perhaps. So you refuse to pursue this line of inquiry?"

"I do, sir. I have hired *you* to make the ghost go away. Can you do so, or not?"

"A few more questions, and then we shall see, Your Grace. I recall that your son was once the subject of a kidnap attempt. Can you tell me of his current whereabouts? It may be pertinent to the case."

A look of distaste fell over the dowager's countenance, but she answered. "I have not seen my son, William Cecil Arthur Clayton, since before he departed on an African expedition almost twenty years ago. He returned in 1910 with an American bride, Miss Jane Porter of Baltimore, but would not see me. He is now the 7th Duke of Holdernesse, but he and his family have never visited Pemberley, and spend most of their time at their estate in Africa."

"Gone native, they say. Swings from the trees and everything," Moran smirked, then shut his mouth at a sharp look from the dowager.

"Do you have any other children?" Blake continued.

"No, only an adopted son."

"His name and whereabouts?"

"His name is Carlo Deguy. I took him in after his parents died. He is currently studying at Cambridge."

"Thank you, duchess. Are there not any other Darcys in the area whom we might enlist?"

This time Moran replied, "No, his lordship the 6th Duke purchased Pemberley House from his cousin, Sir Gawain Darcy, who had purchased it from Fitzwilliam Bennet Darcy (the son of Fitzwilliam Darcy and Elizabeth Bennet) when that gentleman experienced great financial difficulties. Fitzwilliam Bennet did have a daughter, Athena, who married the 6th Duke's brother, the 5th Duke of Holdernesse. However, that line died out in 1888 when the 5th Duke's son, John Clayton, and his pregnant wife Alice were lost at sea when the *Fuwalda* went down off the shores of the island of St. Helena."

"Mr. Moran, you seem to know quite a bit of the Clayton family history," Blake remarked.

"I should. It's part of my own family history. John Clayton served with my grandfather in East India in 1883."

"Ah, your grandfather, the famous—some would say infamous—Col. Sebastian Moran!"

The duchess' secretary shrugged.

"Well, then, the *Fuwalda*," Blake continued. "There were no survivors?"

"Oh, there were rumors over the years of ship-wrecked survivors, feral children, raised by apes and so forth. But those rumors came from French Congo, far from St. Helena. Utter rot, of course," Moran said.

"Very well, that line of inquiry seems fruitless. Your Grace, there are no other lineal descendants of the d'Arcys of whom you are aware?" Blake pressed.

A strange look crossed the duchess' face. "No, Mr. Blake, there are not. I have grown quite tired at your impertinence, and cannot fathom how this intrusive line of questioning will solve my present dilemma. I can see now you are not the right man for this particular job. You may leave. Moran, show these men out and bar them from the estate."

"Certainly, Your Grace."

And Augustus Moran did just that.

Moran...The infamous Col. Sebastian Moran. I should know that name...Patricia thought, but she couldn't dredge up the significance.

She was groggy and felt disoriented. She couldn't keep her eyes open and gave up fighting against sleep. She barely reached the switch on the bedside lamp before she dropped off into a deep, deep slumber.

15.

THE ROOM WAS darkened, the curtains pulled completely over the French windows.

Patricia half woke up and felt drugged. It was 12 midnight. The ghost of Bess came toward her. She wore a simple cotton night gown, and her flowing dark hair offset a snow white complexion and red lips.

A tiny part of Patricia's mind orbited around her and told her this was Carla.

Bess sat at Patricia's bedside and kissed her deeply. She pulled down the covers to Patricia's waist. The dying fire and embers in the grate cast a warm glow on Patricia's full breasts. Patricia kicked the covers to the foot of the bed. Both Patricia and the ghost were naked now, and Carla's—no, Bess's—dark nipples were hard with anticipation. She pulled Patricia's mouth down to her right breast and lightly ran her fingers along Patricia's inner thigh. Then she gently pushed Patricia down into a prone position and kissed her bronzed breasts; her tongue danced in teasing circles around the pink aureole, never quite contacting the nipples. Patricia's blood flowed south and so did Bess's tongue, sliding down her abdomen while smoothly slipping a finger inside her. Bess inched further down and went down on her.

Bess's tongue slid up and down, and around, for what seemed like hours. It penetrated and licked and darted, and Patricia cried out. Her breath came in hard, punctuated gasps and she groaned as the orgasm exploded from a warm spot in her core, her feet and legs going ice-cold.

Then she struggled up out of a haze to hear banging on the door. She staggered out of bed, legs wobbly, and lurched toward the door.

"Patricia, it's me, Parker," the raised voice came, followed by more insistent knocking at the door.

Patricia's heart raced and she was about to unchain and unbolt the door when she realized she was naked.

"Jus' a minnit," she slurred; her tongue was thick and heavy in her mouth.

"What was that? Patricia, are you all right?" The banging became even more persistent.

"Jus' a damn minnit," she yelled.

She turned around to look for a robe and stared at the bed. The sheets were disheveled and pillows scattered. Otherwise the bed itself was empty. She turned on the table lamp and gazed around the room. She stumbled back toward the hall door and peeked in the bathroom. Empty. She pulled the curtains aside and checked the French windows. Locked from the inside.

Bess was gone.

"Patricia, open up!"

"All right, all right." She slipped on her satin robe, unlocked the door, and opened it a crack.

Parker peered in the narrow gap, concern etched on his face. "Patricia, what the hell is going on?"

"Thas Lady Wildman to you, Pete, an whas it to you, anyway?"

"Sorry. Lady Wildman it is. Are you drunk? Is someone in here? Miss Neston heard cries from your room and summoned me."

Patricia flung the door open with a flourish and it banged against the wall with a loud crack. No doorstops in an old place like this. She'd have to have them installed when she took it over, she thought, but said, "No one here but me an' the ghost, Pete. C'mon in, shee for yourself. Whadda you care, anyway...?"

"You and the ghost? Patricia, there's no one here."

"You think I don' know that, Pete?"

"Patricia, what's going on? If you're not drunk, then something else is wrong with you."

"Nah, I'm jus' a heavy shleeper, thas all, Pete."

"Fine, have it your way. Just do me a favor, and make sure to lock up tight behind me."

"Shure thing, Pete, shure thing." She closed the door, walked away, then remembered, shambled back and locked up, and tumbled into bed.

As she drifted off, Patricia ran her hands up and down her arms, massaged her breasts, felt herself down lower. She found she was wet between the legs, the result of her wet dream—if it was a wet dream.

Then she slept again.

16.

ATRICIA HAD SLUMBERED extraordinarily deeply, except for Parker getting her up at all hours. She couldn't stop thinking about Bess-Carla, though she chalked it up to a dream, a very vivid dream, brought on by Carla's flirting and the stories about Bess's ghost.

Still, she was prone to vivid dreams, a result of her boundless imagination and genius intellect. She was also used to sex dreams, although in the past they had usually been about her father, or occasionally and more recently, Denis. She had never dreamed about another woman before. Technically, that wasn't true, she corrected herself. Rather, she would dream about her father and mother making love, observing them unseen from a hidden doorway or window, or from an impossible vantage point floating above them. Then she would invariably become an active participant, entering the dream and displacing her mother as it progressed.

In the dreams, her father would explain that it was wrong and that he would get help for her. She had to get over her complex, her obsession, grow up. Her fixation on him also hurt her mother. She needed treatment.

However, it was her dream. She controlled it. Thus, he'd keep on thrusting, deep into her core. He was behind her. On top of her. Then she was on top. Always she came in shudders and gasps, waking up to drenched bedcovers.

Like she had last night.

She had been intelligent and self-aware enough to understand, clinically, that she had a problem. Her father had gotten her the best doctors, the best psychologists. She was high-functioning, and her hang-up with her father hadn't interfered with most aspects of her life. Still, no one had been able to help her. And she had a hard time banishing her father from her thoughts when she had sex.

She had been grateful, at least, that her obsession with her father didn't prevent her from having orgasms with her sexual partners. Although she hadn't had a very good one when she had lost her virginity to Clive. Her experience with Helen Benson the following year had truly awakened her, sexually, and after that she had fulfilling sexual experiences with several men, though still always colored by and contrasted with her fantasies about her father, whom she always visualized while with other men. And to be honest, not just her fantasies, for it would be very hard indeed for any man to compare favorably to her father, in any way, intellectually, physically, or sexually.

After Helen, Patricia didn't have any other encounters with women—until Pemberley—even though it was Helen who first succeeded in bringing her to orgasm while she wasn't fantasizing about her father or comparing her partner to him.

And her dream the prior night—it could only have been a dream—in which her father played no part, had left her entirely satisfied and fulfilled.

Her father and mother were dead. But for the first time, she grieved for her father without the sensation of loss of a lover, but rather a parent. She grieved equally for her mother. She wanted her mother back, rather than fantasizing about getting rid of her, sending her somewhere far away, so she could have her father to herself. She cried a little as she thought of her parents, and felt better for letting it out.

She was energized this morning and decided to dress to kill. She put on a black lace garter belt, and attached sheer black back-seamed stockings with Cuban heels, rolling them slowly up tanned legs which went on forever. She slipped on a low-cut white blouse and pulled it tight over her breasts. Taking a move out of Carla's playbook, she skipped a brassiere. A black skirt and her black leather "kinky boots," a present from one of her tutors, Mrs. Gale, completed the ensemble. She headed downstairs, refreshed and ready to handle whatever the day threw at her.

The conversation at breakfast centered on the seventh duke's will, which was to be read in two days. Patricia was not concerned. She knew the contents pretty well. She was another day closer to inheriting and then she'd deal with the rotten core infesting Pemberley House.

The others at the table also knew at least the general provisions of the will. Their attitudes about it didn't make her feel particularly welcome. Richard, in particular, was unpleasant to her, but by now that was nothing new.

She decided to confront him. "Richard, it's obvious you find me objectionable and disagreeable. Is it because I've failed to succumb to your charms?"

Carla, and even the old duchess, could not hide small smirks.

"Or do you somehow see me as standing in your way as the next lord and master of this estate?"

The old lady's expression turned sour and a collective hush settled over the table.

"Because I have to tell you," Patricia plowed on, "I am conversant with the terms of the will, and as it has been explained to me by competent legal counsel, acting entirely in my interest, there is no possible way for you to inherit Pemberley House."

"How dare you—"

"I dare, Mr. Deguy, because of your consistent rude and boorish behavior incompatible with that of a proper English gentleman. On top of which, you appear to be frighteningly unacquainted with the system of titles of nobility and descent known as the peerage. You seem to operate under some sort of fantasy that with me out of the way—whether by scaring me off in girlish tears with your ghost stories, or repulsing me into leaving to avoid your unwanted advances—your path to a dukedom will be clear upon your grandmother's passing.

"Allow me to disabuse you of your ill-conceived notions. We all perfectly understand the venerable duchess is your grandmother by adoption only. But by your actions and attitude, I can only conceive you operate under some delusion that if you succeed in disposing of me, you will become a Peer of the Realm, despite your lack of a blood relationship. You, sir, are the son of an adopted son. You might inherit this house and this land from your adoptive grandmother if I was out of the way, but in no case can you aspire to nobility. Period. Furthermore, you will not take hold of Pemberley House and Pemberley Woods, because I am not leaving. I am staying right here and taking that to which I'm entitled.

"Therefore, I entreat you, sir, in front of these people—your grandmother, your sister, the good doctor—to cease your ill-mannered and abusive treatment and accord me the civilized conduct which a cousin, even an American cousin by adoption, could reasonably expect."

A palpable silence had engulfed the table's inhabitants. The morning sun's rays beat in and dust motes floated in the stillness. The clock in the corner ticked off the seconds.

Then from the duchess: "Good show, well done, my dear."

"Yes. Very Jane Austen," Carla added with a wink and a knowing grin.

Moran nodded, and Richard, amazingly, appeared remorseful. "You're right, of course, coz, I've been an awful beast. Stress of last few days, I'd say. Of course that's no excuse, and I apologize."

Patricia nodded her acceptance, but the duchess interrupted. "Stress of the last few days? What stress?" she demanded.

Before anyone else could reply, Patricia cut in. "I imagine, Your Grace, my arrival has stirred up emotions about the seventh duke's recent passing which had only started to heal. Everyone must be under a terrible strain."

Richard stared at her as if she had just landed from another planet. Even Carla looked bemused.

"Pray continue, child."

"I only wish to reassure you, Your Grace, and everyone else, that I took your admonitions the other day quite seriously. I will of course do everything in my power, once Pemberley legally passes to me, to ensure the happiness and tranquility of yourself and your grandchildren. And Doctor Moran, of course. I cannot envision any situation or occurrence in which anyone will be able to discern, on any level, the change in legal ownership. Everyone shall continue to live their lives at Pemberley as they did before my arrival, in any manner they see fit. Is that perfectly clear?"

"Oh, my child, I knew it," the old lady said. "I knew you would understand and fulfill your familial obligations. I am fully satisfied."

Richard still stared at her, dumbfounded. Moran mustered up an avuncular grin. Carla smiled and shook her head in admiration.

"I am glad," Patricia said. "Now, if you'll excuse me everyone, I have a bit of reading I'm dying to catch up on."

Patricia tossed her napkin on the table and walked out. That ought to stir them up.

17.

S IT TURNED out, Patricia didn't catch up on her reading that morning. The sun was bright and the spring day was clear, so she decided to take a walk around the lake and through dark oaks of the woods. She hiked up the rise to the Mary's Tower. She walked slowly around the base of the circular structure, imagining herself a Lilliputian woman sauntering around Gulliver's giant shaft, and laughed softly.

Revitalized, she returned to her room early in the afternoon. She picked up the Saxon Blake magazine, eager to continue the story, and found the spot at which she had left off; Moran had just booted Blake and Topper from Pemberley at the duchess' behest.

"She's lying, Topper, I'm certain of it."

Safely ensconced back at Baker Street, Saxon Blake and Topper were reviewing the case.

"About the *Fuwalda*, guv'nor? You dropped that line of questioning pretty abruptly."

"No, Topper, she doesn't know anything about that, which is doubtless for the best."

"Why's that?"

Blake gestured at the wall covered in leather binders of case files, many of which he had inherited from Holmes when the latter had retired. "I know the real story of the *Fuwalda*, Topper. One of Holmes' unpublished cases. An adventure he and Watson had in Africa in 1916. Technically he's still under retainer, and since I've carried on his practice, I'm also bound by confidentiality on the case."

Topper looked bewildered.

"Topper, suffice to say, there was a survivor from the *Fuwalda*, who *was* 'raised by apes,' Moran's mockery notwithstanding. The boy looked much like his cousin, William Cecil Arthur Clayton, the duchess' son—who died in Africa in 1910."

"Guv'nor!"

"Yes, and when William Cecil died, the young man assumed his cousin's identity and title—a lordship he was entitled to assume anyway, mind you. That is why he refuses to see the duchess. She is probably the one person alive who can expose him, besides Holmes and us, of course."

"Why did he do it?"

"To avoid publicity and hounding by the press, old son."

"But the duchess thinks her son is alive. We have to tell her!"

"No, Topper, in this case, Holmes' client—the current Duke of Holdernesse—must also be treated as our client. Confidentiality binds us. The current duke is a descendent of the Darcys, but that avenue is closed. Don't feel too badly for Her Grace, in any case. As I said, she is lying to us."

"But guv', what can we do?" asked Topper. He was no slouch as an investigator in his own right, but he couldn't see his way through this problem.

Blake made no reply, though, retreating to the settee and filling the sitting room with bilious pipe smoke as he pondered the problem. This went on for hours, the lean detective only stirring to replenish his bowl.

Finally, Blake's ruminations came to a sudden halt when the detective jumped up with a cry and snatched the evening *Globe* out of Topper's hands.

"That's it!" he exclaimed, turning the paper back to the front page and spreading it out on the table.

"But what, guv'nor, what?"

"This, old son," said Blake, and pointed to one of the headlines, which read:

AMERICAN DOCTOR LAUNCHES ASIATIC EXPEDITION

Doctor Francis Ardan of New York City announced his intention today to mount an expedition to the Koko Nor in the Kunlun region of Mongolia. Ardan, who received his M.D. from Johns Hopkins last year, is also a renowned scientific researcher, with advanced degrees in several different disciplines. The stated purpose of the expedition is to investigate the region's vast, untapped mineral resources. Ardan is a veteran of a 1925 Antarctic expedition and exploration is in his blood. In 1917-18, Ardan's father, along with the celebrated Hareton Ironcastle, led an expedition in search of the so-called "Lost World" in South America, first identified by Professor George Edward Challenger and Lord John Roxton. Ardan's father is also credited with opening up significant trade routes into the interior of British Hidalgo.

The younger Ardan plans to launch his journey to the mysterious Orient from Croydon Aerodrome in South London next week, equipped with...

"Yes, yes, I've been a fool. Should've reviewed all the particulars of the Priory School case immediately," muttered Blake to himself. He slapped the paper down and strode to the vast bookcase which covered one whole wall of their lodgings. His keen mind working, he selected a volume from the Ws of the *Baker Street Index and Case-books* and began to rapidly flip the pages. Harrumphing with triumph, Blake snapped the book shut, went to the telephone, and requested an exchange in Sussex, once again conferring with his old friend, Sherlock Holmes.

* * *

The three men, Saxon Blake, Topper, and Doctor Francis Ardan had been made to wait nearly an hour before they were finally admitted to an audience with Edith, Duchess of Holdernesse. The lavish surroundings did little to pass the time, although Ardan did take an especial interest in the 6th Duke's portrait as they were escorted through the Great Hall and into the presence of the duchess and her secretary.

Blake observed they were both a bit flushed. He thought it wholly improper—she was 58, after all, while Moran was a mere lad of 20—but dismissed the line of thought as none of his business. Perhaps he was wrong; it was rather muggy in the hothouse.

"Mr. Blake, I have discharged you from the case. By what right do you present yourself here today?" the duchess demanded. Her tone was laced with acid.

"May it please Your Grace, I have not yet returned your retainer, and therefore technically am still in your employ. I should like to introduce Doctor Francis Ardan of New York City."

Ardan was a tall man, almost 6 foot 8, but was so well proportioned, his size didn't strike one all at once. His skin was bronzed, his hair a shade darker, and tiny gold flecks seemed to swirl in his eyes. A patrician nose, high forehead, and square jaw completed the picture.

The duchess was taken aback in spite of herself. "Well, I suppose, that is..." she smiled, like a cat who'd caught the canary. "I am very pleased to meet you, Doctor."

"A doctor, eh?" Augustus Moran interjected, with perhaps a hint of jealousy, and puffed himself up. "I'm pursuing a medical degree myself."

Ardan nodded politely, while the dowager shushed Moran. The secretary sat back down, properly chastised, a slow burn creeping up past his collar.

"Mr. Blake, my question still stands. Why are you here?"

"A most valid question, duchess. I am here, with Doctor Ardan's assistance, to solve your little ghost problem."

"And how, pray tell, do you intend to do that?"

"You will recall the incident of your son's kidnapping from the Priory School? That was in 1901, correct?"

"Of course, although I was not in the country at the time."

"The reason for your estrangement from your husband—"

"—is entirely my own."

"Forgive me, Your Grace, but you have not been completely open with me. You were estranged from your husband due to the presence in this household of his illegitimate son, a man you knew as James Wildman, who participated in the kidnapping of your son, his half-brother."

"How dare you—!"

Blake plowed on. "Furthermore, this man," he gestured to Francis Ardan, "is the son of the aforementioned Mr. Wildman, who was known to use several aliases—Savage and Ardan, to name but two—in the wake of his hasty departure from England with his pregnant wife. Thus Ardan here is a lineal descendent of the Darcys. I have brought him to help put an end to the curse."

"Get out! Get out!" she shrieked. "Moran, get them out!"

"Curse?" asked Ardan. "You didn't say anything about a curse."

"Please, please! Everyone, quiet please, calm yourselves," Blake said. Slowly the group settled, although the duchess was clearly mortified. "Your Grace, do you wish to dispense with these ghostly midnight visitations or not?"

She took a deep breath before replying, "I do."

"Very good, then. According to the legend, Bess should appear at midnight tomorrow night, to a descendant of the Darcys. As the grandson of your late husband, Doctor Ardan is such a descendant."

"This is inconceivable."

"I understand," Blake nodded, "you don't wish to burden Doctor Ardan with your troubles. Laudable sentiments, indeed! Shall we call in his father, then? He'd do as nicely."

"That Lothario? I'd die before allowing him in this house again," spewed the duchess. She turned, addressing Ardan. "You know, of course, what a scoundrel he is!"

"My father carries enormous guilt for the kidnapping of your son, and has made every effort to atone by doing good and charitable works, duchess. He's a good man, whatever his past," said Ardan.

"Perhaps, but I imagine he never told you about the Lambton tavern wenches. Your mother wasn't the first—"

Ardan blushed. "Your Grace, with respect, no one wishes to hear about their parents'…er, romantic escapades, least of all me. It makes me feel very, well...awkward. I came here today at Mr. Blake's behest, to help you, not subject myself to your tirades about my father. I'd be just as happy to leave, now. So at the risk of repeating Mr. Blake's question, do you wish our help or not?"

She nodded, tightly.

"Right then, Doctor Ardan, you *are* still game?" Saxon Blake asked.

The American nodded, slowly. "I don't believe in curses, or ghosts, and by the way, you brought me here under false pretences."

Blake had the good grace to look embarrassed, but Ardan continued. "However, I'm intrigued. As long as this doesn't interfere with the departure of my expedition next week, I'll play along. What do I have to do?"

"Yes, guv'nor, tell us!" interjected Topper.

"Simple. Be here at Pemberley House tomorrow night at midnight. That's the first of the three nights of the curse, and it's my hope only one night will be necessary."

"That's fine," Ardan replied evenly, "but is that it? What do I do when the ghost—not that I believe in ghosts, mind you—appears?"

"The legend goes that the ghost of Bess will depart if she is shown love, not terror and hatred..."

"Yes, so, what am I to do, tell the ghost she's loved? That I love her?" Ardan asked, clearly perplexed.

"Not exactly."

"Then, what?"

"Guv', for heaven's sake, tell us!" said Topper.

"Unlike you, I'm not one easily given to embarrassment, Ardan, but..."

"What?!" everyone in the room yelled in chorus.

There was an insistent knock at Patricia's door. Damn it, she thought, but controlled her impatience at the interruption. It was Miss Neston, come to summon her to an audience with the duchess.

Patricia followed the maid through the archways, corridors and landings, her mind reeling. The man called "Doctor Francis Ardan" in the Blake story was her father. And he actually had been here, at Pemberley House, in 1927. He had never mentioned it, of course, nor had he discussed his own father's past crime and ignominious departure from Pemberley. But he had admitted it to the duchess all those years ago, if the Blake story was accurate and to be believed, and this was confirmation of everything the duchess had told Patricia about her father a few days ago, during their first audience in the hothouse sitting room.

Now Patricia was back in the hothouse again, and the old duchess was reminiscing, with Doctor Moran in attendance. Patricia couldn't keep from thinking about seeing the old doctor and his huge member and Mrs. Abingdon two nights ago. And despite her dream last night, she had a resurgence of sexual feelings. She was pent up. She'd only had one sexual experience since her husband was killed, although the encounter with Ernie was as far from pleasurable as it could get.

Or was it two experiences? Did the ghost of Bess last night count, or was it a dream? Patricia didn't believe spirits were real, or at least up till now hadn't believed that they walked among the land of the corporeal, haunting the living. In that respect, as in many others, she was the daughter of her father, through and through.

Her father, Doc Wildman, had been a very rich man; in addition to his medical expertise—he had taken his medical degree at Johns Hopkins and was quickly acknowledged as the world's top surgeon—he was an inventor and a philanthropist, and he also followed in his own father's footsteps, traveling the world and mounting various expeditions.

Above all else, he was a crime fighter.

He had numerous adventures in his lifetime, adventures in which many evil men met their ends, adventures which bordered on the fantastic and surreal. Many times it had appeared that the only explanation for the mysteries he encountered was a supernatural one. And time after time Doc Wildman had prevailed, and debunked the mystical in favor of the rational and scientific.

Despite this, her father did occasionally encounter a few mysteries, and beings, which defied logical explanation.

One such instance was a case in the late 1940s that brought her father and mother together. Her father denied to Patricia that the case had had any occult trappings, but her mother had once taken her daughter aside and told her the story. As her mother told it, it was she who originally had to be convinced by Wildman that there was an actual danger, that the supernatural aspects of the case were real.

Her mother had understood. "'There are more things in heaven and earth, Horatio...'" she had quoted, and he had agreed.

It wasn't their very first meeting—that had been a month earlier, when Adélaïde Lupin had palmed a priceless jewel, tricked Wildman, and made a clean escape—but even so, she had instinctively trusted this bronze giant, this hero of Technopolis who now implored her to believe in the unexplained. She had placed herself in his hands, and he saved her life, although barely.

Somewhat more than two years later, Patricia's father had had an exploit which shook him to his core. He had almost always represented himself as a rationalist, a skeptic, a scientist. But in 1948, when he had trailed a man, or what he thought was a man, into a subterranean complex, he had found things he couldn't explain. He might have wandered into the inferno described by Dante, but he couldn't believe that. The weird forms of life weren't the souls of the dead; they couldn't be. There was no such thing as Hell; at least, not the Hell which some postulated.

After his terrifying experiences there, her father had blocked up the entrance. Not to keep the things there from getting out, since that, at least, seemed impossible, but to keep people from going into it. For the first time in his daring life he'd encountered beings whom he didn't risk battling.

This was his last recorded exploit. He had allowed the pulp magazines of the era to publish fictionalized versions of his globe-trotting adventures, and Patricia of course had access to the whole collection. When she had read the tale and asked him about it a few years ago, he had dismissed it. "Focus on the real, the observable, the testable, the provable," he had said.

"What did you observe, then? What came up from Earth's center?" she asked.

"It was just a story, Patricia. My biographers did invent them out of whole cloth, sometimes."

She had never known whether to believe him or not, especially given her previous conversation with her mother. Her father did not retire after that case, if in fact the case had actually happened, but he did scale back his crime-busting activities a bit, and even more so the following year when he married Patricia's mother.

When Patricia had told her mother of her father's dismissal of the supernatural, her mother continued to insist that the adventure in the subterranean complex had really occurred, and what's more that her father had had other experiences which his rationalism couldn't explain. When he was a young man, during the Great War, he had observed a long whitish worm crawling over the skeleton of an infant, a victim of a satanic ritualistic sacrifice. He was never able to classify the worm, and it remained unknown to science. In 1925, he had encountered an entity which slaughtered most of an Antarctic expedition. He had had no explanation. In 1927, he had observed an Asian doctor, the megalomaniac head of the worldwide Si-Fan criminal organization, transmute lead into gold; he was never able to reproduce the feat by any scientific means. In 1929, one of his colleagues, a geologist and archaeologist named Doctor Littlejohn, had also traveled to the Antarctic, and had strange experiences which he, also a rational man of science, could not explain. In 1943, he had been involved in a case in which an herbal concoction allowed its taker to see into the future; a specific prophecy had come true.

When Patricia had confronted her father with all this, he told her it was all fiction. And so Patricia was never sure if her mother was teasing her or not.

Then the old duchess' conversation penetrated Patricia's brain, and she forgot, temporarily at least, her own worries about whether what happened last night, and whether Bess's ghost, was, or could be, real or not.

The old duchess was talking about her love affair with the Prince of Wales, later King Edward VII, which Carla and Richard had told Patricia about the other day, and Edward's liking for perversions, which they hadn't. The duchess had been one of the Prince's many mistresses, at least for a short time. Others had been Lillie Langtry, Lady Randolph Churchill, Sarah Bernhardt, Carolina Otero (known as *La Belle Otero*), and Agnes Keyser.

"How did it turn out, Duchess?" It was obvious Moran had heard it all before, but was keeping the old lady talking for Patricia's benefit.

"Well, there were letters, of course."

"Of course."

"And then it ended."

"Yes?"

"And I married the Marquess Blackwater."

"When was that?"

"Oh, this would have been, let's see…1885. I was sixteen."

"Sixteen, and you had already conducted one affair with the Prince of Wales, and then married a Marquess."

"Oh yes, things happened at a much faster pace in those days. Girls married much younger, before they lost their youth and were regarded as spinsters. You had to pounce, act decisively, to make an appropriate match."

"But you weren't married to the Marquess for long."

"No. He died."

"What happened?"

"The letters. The damned letters. The reptile—I call him the reptile—got hold of them."

"Blackmail?" Doctor Moran made sympathetic noises, though this was nothing new to him.

"Yes. Blackmail."

"And?"

"I couldn't pay. He showed the letters to my husband. The Marquess was heartbroken."

"But the affair with Prince Edward, it happened before you married the Marquess, didn't it?"

"Of course. But it was different then. I was not a virgin." The old woman emerged from her reverie and addressed Patricia. "You girls have it much easier these days. The Marquess was devastated. He killed himself over the shame of it."

"I'm so sorry," Patricia said. This was the second conversation with the duchess in her hothouse rooms where she found herself empathizing with the dowager and her losses, despite her dislike for the old woman. But then, anyone who lived as long as she had would have experienced losses.

"Don't be. I was heartbroken then. A dumb, silly girl. It was, what, how long, Moran?"

The doctor did a quick mental calculation. "Almost 88 years ago, Your Grace."

"88 years ago. Well, an appallingly long time ago, and now time and distance and loss of pain have done their work, destroyed my love. He was pathetic. Why should he have killed himself just because I had an affair, and especially with the greatest man in England? And before I even got married; I was faithful after marriage, but his suicide was a terrible act of faithlessness to me. So I see things differently now, my dear. I don't need your sorrow. Anyway, I vowed vengeance, although I had to wait years for it. And when I heard that the reptile was blackmailing a friend of mine, I returned from the South of France and shot him dead, emptying six bullets into him."

Patricia was shocked.

"Don't look so surprised, dear. I found out later that somebody else had been there and robbed the safe. Two burglars got blamed for the murder, and they escaped the police. And what can anybody do about it now?" A malevolent, scratching noise came from the duchess' mouth; it was laughter. "I'll deny it if you tell. It was 74 years ago, so who cares now? Even that bastard detective back in '27—what was his name, Moran? Black?—even he couldn't do anything about it."

Patricia was appalled, and also wondered why the duchess told her all this. To scare her into leaving now and renouncing her inheritance? If so, the old bitch was doing a good job of it, but she wasn't leaving. This house was, if not evil, filled with a history of ancient evil and with living evil people: the duchess, Austin, Doctor Moran, and Richard, who was up to no good. Even Carla, whom she liked, was covering up what she and Richard had been doing the other night.

Why could the house not have had wonderful people as it did two-hundred years ago, people like Fitzwilliam Darcy and Elizabeth Bennet? Like Charles and Jane Bingley? But even back then, the house had its bad apples, such as George Wickham, if Jane Austen's book about Patricia's distant ancestors was to be believed. Now, the only good people were the butler, the maid, and maybe the gamekeeper.

"What's the matter dear, cat got your tongue?" the old lady inquired.

Patricia stared at her.

"That was a nice bit of flowery language you spouted this morning at breakfast. I didn't believe a word of it. I'll have you out of here before I die, if it's the last thing I do. I take care of people who cross me, do you understand?"

Patricia continued to watch her and didn't respond.

"Do you understand me?" The duchess shrieked. Spittle flew out of her shriveled mouth and she started to spasm and jerk.

Moran glared at Patricia, venom in his eyes. "You'd better—"

But Patricia was already up and walking out, just like she had two days ago. Déjà vu all over again.

She stopped and turned in the doorway. "By the way, Your Grace. Richard and Carla are dying to know what you're keeping from them. You may want to let them know you're a cold-blooded murderess. I think Richard, at least, will be impressed. Oh, and I understand why everyone has been trying to scare me off with the stories about Bess of Pemberley; I'm descended from the d'Arcys, so I'm supposedly cursed. But why are you so afraid? Must be that Hungarian count in your bloodline from way back who a d'Arcy married, hmm? Oh, and the detective's name was Blake, not Black. Ciao."

Patricia waved and strode out of the hothouse. She could hear the duchess screaming accusations at Moran, and his denials, all the way down the hall, and was satisfied.

The old bitch had been right about one thing, though. Patricia had been putting them on at breakfast, just to see what would happen.

Now she knew.

| 18.

ATRICIA WANDERED THE house a bit. She spent some time in the music room playing Georgiana Darcy's pianoforte (like her father, Patricia was also a talented musician), and then contemplated the family portraits in the Great Hall. She stopped in the vast library and browsed the contents of the massive bookshelves for a while. She spent several hours tracing her lineage in Burke's *Peerage*, just to satisfy her curiosity and confirm what she had been told. She also perused Delhi Darcy's *Excessively Diverted*, after which she returned to her bedchamber. She took dinner in her room again that night, the third and final night the ghost of Bess was due to appear.

When Miss Neston delivered the tray of food, Patricia thanked her for the stack of books and magazines she had delivered a few days ago.

"Sorry, ma'am?"

"The books and magazines you put on my night table. It was very thoughtful, thank you."

"Oh, but that wasn't me, ma'am."

"Well, someone brought them into my room when I wasn't here. I just assumed it was you."

"Sorry, ma'am, but it wasn't."

"Who else has access to my room, then?"

The maid thought about it for a moment, then replied, "Nobody. At least, nobody should, ma'am."

Patricia was quiet, until Miss Neston asked, "Will you be wanting anything else, ma'am?"

"No, that's all, you can go."

She wolfed down her dinner. She wanted to finish the Blake detective story—although there was too much truth in it to be just a story, she knew—to discover if it contained any more revelations she could use to her benefit. Apparently Blake had, all those years ago, discovered the duchess' murderous ways, although Patricia had not yet reached that part of the tale.

To her chagrin, she discovered the magazine was gone. She searched everywhere in her room, but it was nowhere to be found. She was disturbed. Someone had to have come into her room to take the magazine, unless Miss Neston had palmed it while she delivered the dinner.

She wished she had known the magazine was gone; she would have looked for it while she was in the library. But she wasn't going to venture out of her room tonight, so she resolved to check the library tomorrow.

Robbed of her preferred reading material, she picked up Sade's *Justine*. She had never read it before. The abuses heaped on the title character, a young French girl, were too reminiscent of the night of her arrival at Pemberley and she tossed the book aside in disgust.

Patricia was restless. She wandered the room and on a lark began tapping the walls, since she'd heard from Parker, and also had read in many guidebooks, that many secret passageways were used by dwellers during religious persecutions, royalist roundhead civil war days, and since then. If someone delivered and removed the reading material, perhaps they were using a secret door to enter and exit. A secret entrance was also the only explanation for Carla's midnight appearances in her room, assuming Bess was not real.

Patricia looked under the bed, inspected the floor for any ill-fitting boards, and even checked behind the huge mirror mounted opposite her bed. But she found nothing suspicious, no sliding panels, no peep holes, and no trap doors.

She rang for tea before bed.

Miss Neston brought the tea, stoked the fire in the grate, lowered the lights, and turned down the bed. Patricia locked the door behind her, sipped her tea, and tried to read again, the Swinburne poetry this time, but the restlessness had deserted her and she couldn't keep her eyes open. The printed words went in and out of focus. She staggered over to the bed and collapsed on her back, fully clothed. She fell asleep at once, dead to the world.

⊷⫸◉⫷⊶

It was midnight. A storm whipped up the wind and rattled the windows.

Patricia was sprawled on the bed, arms akimbo and legs splayed, one booted foot pointing at the gilt-edged mirror facing the bed, the other hanging off the bedside.

Lightning crashed. Patricia awoke with a start, eyes wide.

Bess stood at the foot of the bed, naked.

Patricia was paralyzed. She could only stare at Bess's alabaster skin, and full, firm breasts. Once again Patricia was stricken; was this Bess or was it Carla? She looked like Carla and yet she didn't, somehow.

Bess —Patricia couldn't think of this apparition as Carla, no matter how hard she tried—came to Patricia, climbing over the foot of the bed. Her eyes blazed. She inched toward Patricia, crawling up between her spread legs. Patricia tried to close them, and Bess stopped her with one hand on each thigh, forcing them apart.

Then Bess lay atop Patricia, nose-to-nose, and Patricia could feel Bess's warm flesh. Dazed, she wondered why a ghost's flesh would be warm. Strong arms gripped Patricia's shoulders, holding her down. Bess's knee insistently rubbed up and down against Patricia's pelvis, and Bess buried her face in Patricia's hair, kissing and nipping at the nape of her neck and earlobes.

Patricia felt like she was outside her body, watching the two lovers, Bess and herself, from a distant vantage point. But she was also inside her body at the same time, grinding and writhing with ecstasy against Bess's knee and upper thigh until she came in jerks and shudders.

Bess got up on her knees, still between Patricia's spread legs. She undid Patricia's skirt and pulled it off. Patricia had gone commando that day so next Bess removed Patricia's blouse. She leaned back down and sucked on Patricia' nipples. She moved up and lowered her own breast into Patricia's mouth. Patricia reciprocated, licking her hard nipples and dark aureole.

Bess moaned.

Patricia, standing outside of herself and watching, considered whether ghosts moaned. Of course they did, she realized. Moaning was a ghost's stock-in-trade. But typically it was moaning and groaning to scare people off, not in response to pleasures one would have thought were restricted to the living and breathing. Also, there were no stereotypical rattling chains dragging across the wooden floor with Bess, and no white sheets. Or rather, this ghost was mussing up the bed's white sheets rather than wearing one.

Patricia, the Patricia who was in bed with Bess, grabbed Bess's derriere and pulled her closer. Bess turned around, lowered herself back to Patricia's waiting lips, and buried her head between Patricia's legs. The two lovers engaged in a vigorous *soixante neuf*, their sighs and soft cries filling the cold room.

Patricia wrapped her legs around Bess's arching torso and squeezed, her boots pressing down on the small of Bess's back. She came again and again in convulsions of orgasms, waves of hot and cold, and then Bess came as Patricia continued to tongue and lick her.

The two women lay together for a while in a tight embrace, heads still between each other's legs, and Patricia began to drift off in post-coital bliss.

Then Bess was not on top of her, but stood at the foot of the bed again, in front of the large mirror, reaching out to Patricia, almost imploringly.

Patricia blinked.

Bess was gone.

Patricia jumped up. She was dizzy, disoriented, and she wanted to follow—follow where, though?—but the ghost was gone.

In a rush, she pulled her skirt and blouse back on and exited her room into the hallway. She looked left and right, but the dimly-lit hall was empty. Just the usual paintings, vases displayed on sideboards, and other objects-de-art that characterized the house.

Patricia was frightened. The ghost had been real. Real flesh and blood. Real skin, hair, eyes, and lips. Real, living people did not just disappear in the blink of an eye.

She had looked for secret entrances and hadn't found any. And even if there was a secret entrance and exit from Patricia's room, there wasn't time for any normal human being to utilize it in an eye-blink.

If Bess was not a normal human being, what was she? Her skin was warm, her heart beat. Patricia had felt it. Spirits were supposed to be ethereal, non-corporeal. One could put a hand right through a ghost and it would come out the other side. Or at least it was that way in films and stories. What was she thinking? What did anyone really know about the spirit world, anyway? If there even was such a thing.

Patricia felt like she was moving in slow motion now, racing toward the stairway to the right of her room at a snail's pace. She was fifteen feet, fifteen yards, fifteen miles from the top of the stairs.

She blinked, and suddenly was at the edge of the stairway. Something caught against her ankles, a cord maybe, then it was gone and she was falling down, and she was being carried, and the butler and Mrs. Abingdon appeared, and everything went black.

| 19.

ATRICIA CAME OUT of her swoon. Red blotchy skin
filled her field of vision. Broken veins criss-crossed
and wove in and around bumps like rivulets flow-
ing around hills and through valleys. The veins disappeared into
thatches of unkempt, sandy grey whiskers. Fleshy lips opened
and closed, revealing yellowed and blackened teeth, jutting and
crooked like stalagmites and stalactites.

Doctor Moran hovered over her, and her brain kicked in,
processing the gibberish coming from the tooth-packed orifice as
words. She wished, however, that he would hurry up. The words
"Are you quite all right now, my dear?" took him two minutes
to utter. She'd never heard someone speak so slowly. His voice
sounded just like one of her 45 singles played at 33 rpm.

"Wha…" she gurgled, and felt like she was trying to speak
underwater.

She also wished he'd take his hand out from under her blouse,
which, in her haste, she had only secured by the bottom two
buttons. His fingers kneaded her nipple, and she didn't like it.

"I said, are you quite all right now, my dear?"

"No," poured out of her mouth like molasses. "Shtop…"
She tried to sit up, and got as far as raising her head a few
inches, which took five minutes. She saw that she was stretched

out on a divan in a sitting room off the hallway at the foot of the stairs.

Footsteps boomed like a series of approaching atomic bomb explosions. Moran removed his hand from Patricia's blouse and a moment later—or it must have been a moment later, although it seemed like minutes—the housekeeper, eight feet tall, appeared over her.

"Ah, here's Mrs. Abingdon with your medicine," Moran said. Continuing to move in slow motion, he took the cup from the woman's hands and held it up to Patricia's lips. Patricia should have been able to swat it away, but was almost paralyzed.

"Drink it up, drink, my dear," Moran said, and the liquid went down her throat like thick, hot lava, gagging her. The lava settled in her stomach and hardened into a lump, and she passed out again.

⟿⟾

She dreamed of hands, more than two hands, touching her, sliding over her abdomen and breasts. There were lips on the inside of her knee, tickling her through her stockings, and then they were brushing up her inner thigh, licking and kissing their way upward. A hand held her wrists together and pulled her half on her side. Hands down lower slapped at her bottom. Another hand massaged and teased a nipple, while a mouth was fastened to the other.

Teeth bit, hard.

She gasped and woke up in darkness in her room, eyes snapping open. She sat up, tense, breathing hard. There seemed to be shadowy figures in the room, shifting in and out of focus, leaning over her as she lay in bed, and then backing away off the bed.

Whereas earlier she had felt like she was speaking underwater, she now heard hissing, whispered voices that sounded like they were underwater.

"Shit, what did you do that for, you woke her up."

"Well, he said she'd be dead to the world all night, how was I to know?"

"Come on, before she really comes out of it…"

Then the shadows were gone, and she knew it had to be by a secret door, since she could see the hall door to her room by the moonlight and nobody exited through it.

Of course, Bess's ghost also came and went from Patricia's room at will, but only at midnight. It was long after midnight and the storm had broken up; the moon shined through in patches. Besides, there were two shadows.

No, it hadn't been Bess. Two people had been in her room, watching her, fondling her, and that meant a secret entrance.

She tried to get up and found she was still very sluggish. She lay back against the down pillows and her breathing stabilized as oxygen pumped through her body. Her fingertips and toes tingled and she started to feel more in control of her body, as if she might be able to move a little bit without the room rotating around her.

Then the lock in the hall door clicked and the door swung inward. In the moonlight, she saw a man come in. He had a walrus moustache and he was naked, his enormous member hanging there like a bell-pull with tiny snakes slithering down it, and she knew it was Doctor Moran.

He came to her bed, climbed on it, and leaned over her on his knees. A drop of something wet landed on her bare stomach, and she realized he was drooling. "Magnificent body, magnificent. Shame to waste it…"

He chuckled, a dry crackling noise, and scooted down to the foot of the bed, grabbing her ankle and pulling her legs apart.

Patricia acted. She sat up in a flash and, though it revolted her to do so, she grabbed his rising penis in her hand and twisted.

Moran screamed and rolled off the bed, and hit the ancient wooden floor with a thud. He continued to roll and writhe in agony.

Patricia jumped off the bed and kicked him, the toe of her boot sinking deep in his huge belly paunch. She straddled his chest, grabbed him by the throat with her left hand, and slammed a hard right into his bulbous nose, sending blood running down his face.

Moran head-butted her on the forehead and, while she was dazed, flipped her off him onto her back. She was coming out of the cocktail of various potions he had given her much sooner than expected, but she was still wobbly and disoriented enough that he was able to punch her in the face before she could react.

Patricia fell back, stunned, her head swimming, and Moran ran out of the room. He returned moments later, now wearing a dressing gown and carrying his medical bag. Injured and furious, he knelt beside her, pulled out a syringe, and, as she raised her head slightly and began to come out of her daze, slipped the needle into her vein.

20.

I**T WAS DARK**, and Patricia was outside. There was the faintest hint of light in the east, however, and she could feel the morning dew which hung over the vast grounds cling to her bare skin.

She was being carried. Two hands hefted her aloft by her knees, another pair of hands under her armpits. She somehow sensed she was being lugged feet-first. There was much grunting and low cursing.

"Bloody idiot. Thought you'd come and help yourself, huh?"

"Well, look at her, Richard, you've been panting after her," Moran said. "Wouldn't you do the same? In fact, I'm surprised you didn't. You knew as well as I did I'd been doping her up."

"As a matter of fact," a third voice said, a woman's, "we had the same idea earlier. Unfortunately, your doping didn't work as well as you thought."

Carla.

"Well, you could've warned me," Moran said. "She did some serious damage."

"Maybe you should go to a *doctor*." Richard guffawed. "Besides, it's your own damn fault for not making the cocktail strong enough to keep her out. And on top of that, you've been banging poor

Mrs. Abingdon blue. Who'd have thunk an old geezer like you had it in you to even consider doing two in a night?"

"You can laugh about it, Richard," Carla said, "but I'm not very happy with the good doctor. He knows I wanted her for myself. I feel a bit cheated by his attempt on her."

"What do you care, Carla? The plan has always been to do away with her. You weren't any more successful getting into her pants than Richard, and even if you were, it's not like you could have kept her around. Not and inherit the money and the estate too, after the old lady goes."

"Doctor, you talk too much."

"It doesn't really matter now." Moran wheezed with the effort of carrying Patricia, then continued speaking. "She's in a waking haze, and even if some part of her brain can hear and process what we're saying, the drugs I've given her ensure she can't connect conscious thought to physical action and reaction. Essentially, I've short-circuited her brain."

"Ah, let the doc blather on if he wants, sis. All he cares about is his reward, a nice solid pension after we inherit, and making sure he's still got Mrs. Abingdon and nice steady stream of women to keep his pipes clean and well-oiled. Hey, Carla, maybe you'll help keep him happy, shag him too, eh?"

"I'd sooner fuck Mrs. Abingdon," she said.

Moran stopped and put his end of the load down, breathing hard. Patricia's head, shoulders, and upper torso rested on the damp grass, while her legs were still elevated under Richard's arms.

"What the hell are you doing, doc?"

"Can't carry her much further…" He was panting.

"Well, get her up off the grass and over on that gravel pathway," Carla said. "She's crushing the grass, we don't want any marks. Jesus, I go to the trouble getting us slippers wrapped in towels to cover our passage on the gravel paths, with a rake to expunge our footprints behind us, and then you go and dump her on the grass. I thought your grandfather was a criminal mastermind, or something."

"No, he was an assassin." Moran managed a smile though his raspy breathing. "He only worked for a criminal mastermind."

"Well, our grandfather was also a master criminal," Richard said.

"Richard, stuff it," Carla said. "We don't have time for a history lesson."

"Richard was kind enough to allow an old man to blather on." Moran puffed with exertion. "Might as well return the favor, I can't heft her again for a few more minutes. Have you tried? She's six feet tall; you'd never know it from her perfect figure, but she must weigh at least twenty-five pounds more than she looks. She must have the thickest, strongest bones of any woman I've ever seen. Anyway, it's still dark, no one will see us, and I need a few more minutes."

Carla sighed in acquiescence and squatted down on her haunches. "Richard, at least bend down closer to the ground while we wait for the old man."

Richard did as his sister instructed, but before he could speak, Moran cut in. "You were about to brag that your grandfather was a Vicomte, but that was he was also an adventurer and crook extraordinaire? That the long held story of his accidental death at Palermo was a sham?"

Richard sputtered. Even Carla's face registered shock.

"Of course I knew he was a crook," Moran continued. "I know all of Pemberley's secrets. Keep that in mind. Here's one I'll wager you didn't know. Your grandfather, the self-styled Vicomte? He was the grandson of the Professor, the mastermind to whom my own grandfather hired out his services. Small world."

Carla and Richard now looked stunned.

"Well, I'm feeling much better now, so let's not sit here with our mouths hanging open," Moran said. "Come on, we have work to do before sunup. Shoot Miss Wildman here in the head, dig a pit and bury her, and then make sure the dowager gets her attorneys to Pemberley straightaway before she passes."

Patricia groaned. She could hear everything, but could do nothing. Moran noticed, however, that she was awake.

"Capital, she's coming around a bit, not enough to do anything though."

"So you say," Richard growled. "You thought you had given her enough of the stuff before, and look what happened."

Moran shrugged.

Richard produced a pistol and ordered Patricia to get up. They started walking again, Patricia held at gunpoint, although she was still very drugged and disoriented.

They made it across the wide expanse of manicured lawns, and up and across the gravel paths, with Carla only having to wipe out the prints when they marched across a woody stretch to Queen Mary's Tower. Moran, rejuvenated after the rest stop, led the way. Richard brought up the rear, the gun aimed at the center of Patricia's back.

Patricia noticed Moran was now out of the dressing gown and in his customary attire. He carried a long cylindrical case, which hung from his shoulder by a well-worn but sturdy black leather strap.

In fact, despite it being before sunup, Carla and Richard were also dressed normally, Richard in a grey trousers and shirt, and Carla in a riding outfit, a low-cut blouse with black trousers and jodhpurs tucked into black boots.

Which meant this was all planned, not a last-minute arrangement. As for Patricia, she still wore the black knee-high boots she had on yesterday, along with the same white blouse (although she had had no opportunity to button it back up) and black skirt. Although less than twenty-four hours had passed, it felt like a lifetime ago when Patricia had dressed herself yesterday morning, deciding with an illicit and empowering thrill to skip the underclothes, just as Carla did.

Now, Carla walked alongside Patricia. She tried to slip her arm around Patricia's waist. Before Patricia could react, Carla's hand was up under her skirt and lightly skirted across the bare flesh of her bottom.

Patricia was not too far gone to protest. Carla was vile, fondling her as she was being led off to her death. "Get your hands off me. What's wrong with you? You're about to kill me, and you're trying to cop a feel."

Carla spoke so the others couldn't hear. "It's not like that. I love you, Patricia. Just renounce your claim to Pemberley and you'll live. I'll take the estate and we can be together. I'll take care of you."

Patricia appeared to consider it. "What about Richard and Moran?" she whispered.

"When we get to Mary's Tower, I'll take Richard's gun to cover you when they start to dig your grave. I'll make sure they dig it big enough for two. When they finish digging, a bullet for each of them in the back of the head and it will all be over. We can fill in the dirt, and be back at the house in time for you to place an early morning call to your lawyer renouncing your inheritance."

Patricia couldn't conceal her horror. "Your own brother…"

"He's an idiot and a lush. You know that. He can't be trusted. Sooner or later he'll fuck things up. Better to get him out of the way now. We can blame their disappearance on the poachers."

"But I don't understand. Even if I don't claim the estate, and when the duchess finally dies…"

"Then she'll will it to me. Just let me worry about that. Are you in?"

Patricia thought hard, analyzing the situation. Carla wasn't making sense. Even if they attributed Richard and Moran's disappearance to Ernie and Jack, surely there would be a search, which would turn up the freshly dug grave at Mary's Tower. If by some miracle Carla's plan did succeed, Carla would have to trust Patricia never to squeal or blackmail her. Unless she really believed Patricia was devoted to her, and Patricia had given her no indication of that at all.

But Carla, Patricia now realized, was crazy, nuts, bonkers. Off her rocker. She'd have to be to think she could get away with any part of her scheme. So maybe, in Carla's mind, Patricia did love her as much as she supposedly loved Patricia.

"Patricia," Carla said, "I asked you a question. Are you in?"

"Yes," Patricia said. "I'm in."

Carla gave Patricia's bottom an affectionate squeeze.

"Good." Carla grinned her wolf-grin. "You can prove it once they dig the grave by shooting them yourself."

⋇⇒◐⇐⋇

The early morning party of four approached Mary's Tower. The Tower was a dark, lance-like silhouette against the now purplish skies in the east.

The brightening of the heavens, however, was countered by ominous clouds rolling in on a whipping wind. At least they'd be inside the Tower, and protected from the early morning thunderstorm, by the time the roiling mass arrived.

There was another problem, though.

A flickering glow emanated from one of the Tower windows, intermittently piercing the darkness like a lighthouse beacon.

"What the hell," Richard said.

"Shut up," Carla said. "We'll go up to investigate. Give me your gun."

Richard complied and she made to hand it to Moran. "Use this to guard her," Carla said, gesturing to Patricia.

"Never mind that, I brought my own." The old doctor grinned, and began unscrewing the cap off one end of the long cylinder. He pulled what looked like a long black cane out of the leather case. The cane was slightly bent at one end, which was of a polished wood and appeared to be a handgrip. Moran put the cane's handgrip to his shoulder and waved the other end at Patricia, indicating she should go stand with her back to a nearby tree. He then raised the end of the cane and sighted her forehead.

"Doc, have you lost your mind? Why the hell are you pointing the tip of that old cane at dear old Patricia?" Richard said.

"Not a cane, my boy," Augustus Moran said. A mass of the yellowed snaggleteeth which filled his mouth showed as he grinned. "Grandfather's air-gun. Deadly. Silent." He pointed to the pistol in Carla's hand. "I'd advise you only use that as a last resort. We don't want gunshots attracting attention, right?"

Carla considered this, then nodded in agreement. She tucked the gun in the top of her boot. She pointed at Patricia and spoke to Moran: "Watch her. Make sure she doesn't escape. But don't shoot her unless she makes a break for it."

"Of course, Lady Deguy," Moran said. "You can count on me."

Carla gestured at Richard to follow her, and then turned back to Moran once more. She wiped a bead of sweat off her upper lip and licked it with her tongue. "And keep your hands off her, understand?"

Moran nodded in overdone obsequiousness and watched the two siblings climb up the hill to Mary's Tower and the flickering light.

Then he turned his attention back to Patricia, the air-gun never wavering, and smiled at her.

⊷═◯═⊷

About ten minutes later, there came a slight rustling of tree branches and leaves from the direction of the Tower.

Moran swung the gun toward the noise, but when Patricia jerked forward, the gun swiveled back at her in an instant.

"Back where you were, Baroness Wildman, or I'll blow your brains all over the place."

Patricia leaned back against the tree trunk.

They didn't have to wait long. Carla emerged from the foliage and came to confer with Moran.

"What did you see? Where's Richard?" the doctor asked.

"It's a man and a woman in the Tower with flashlights. Richard stayed behind to keep spying on them," Carla said. "They dug up the dead baby, but they continued digging and found bags full of money and bullion. We overheard them—it's from the Great Train Robbery."

"Dead baby, what dead baby? And how could the loot from the Train Robbery be buried in the Tower?"

"Hold on, one at a time. During that break-in by the poachers the other night, the ones that were after Austin—I guess their names are Ernie and Jack, according to Patricia—Richard and I were out getting his bar-whore Rosamond an abortion. So as we approached the Tower just now, Richard was particularly upset someone had found where we buried the baby the other night."

"My dear, I could have helped—"

"Oh, shut it, you old codger, you would've been blackmailing Richard forever over that."

"Well, yes, there is that, I see your point. So?"

"So we buried the baby in a room under Mary's Tower. We had no idea the Train Robbery money was also buried there. The two we saw digging it up must be Ernie and Jack."

"Then Austin must have been in on the Train Robbery," Moran said. "That sly fox."

"Well, you hired him, doctor. These two, Jack and Ernie, the so-called poachers, must have known Austin was in on it. They've been trying to get to him for weeks. Apparently they sometimes hole up in another room in the Tower, near the one where we buried the baby, never suspecting the money they sought was under their feet, although I guess from what they said their main hideout is nearby in Bakewell or some other village. But last night, when they came back to the Tower, they saw where we'd disturbed the earth floor. They dug down, found the baby's body, and then the money."

"The money..." Moran said.

"The money," Carla agreed.

Still keeping an eye on Patricia, the two mapped out a plan of action.

"Not only can we all get the estate and Richard the title, but also the swag from the Robbery. We'll have to kill those two in the Tower, of course, in addition to her," the doctor said, nodding at Patricia.

"But we'll be rich," Carla said.

"No need to tell the duchess about this, of course."

"Well, of course not. She doesn't know about our plans to dispose of our American cousin here, why should she know about the money? It's not like she can take it with her. All she has to do after Patricia here is dead is present proof about me and Richard, will the estate to us, and then we'll have the estate, Richard the title, and all this money."

"You'll have the estate. Not me. You'd better keep your bargain for the pension we agreed on, and I want a third of this loot—"

"Now, now, doctor, don't get your panties all in a bunch, of course we'll all share equally."

Patricia's mind reeled as she listened to the two argue. The duchess wasn't in on their plans to kill her? Then the old lady really must have believed in the ghost and hoped Patricia would have been scared away by the curse and the veiled threats.

And what was this about presenting some kind of proof which would enable Richard to inherit the title? What sort of proof could change the rules of the peerage?

She also wasn't sure if the mercurial Carla was being disingenuous with the old doctor, and still intended to keep Patricia alive, or if, now that plunder from the Train Robbery had entered the picture, she had changed her mind.

Carla and Moran finished conferring. They ordered Patricia to take the lead and, with Moran covering her from behind with the air-rifle, the three climbed up the hill to the Tower.

21.

W<small>HEN</small> P<small>ATRICIA</small>, C<small>ARLA</small>, and Doctor Moran, drenched from the morning onslaught of rain, arrived at the base of the Tower, an unexpected sight greeted them.

Just outside the entrance stood Richard. A man—his right arm wrapped around Richard's chest and his left hand holding a rather large, very sharp knife at his throat—stood behind him. Purplish bruises darkened the man's cheek and the area around one of his eyes.

Richard's skin was as sheet-white as dead Bess d'Arcy's, the blood drained from his face, and sweat was pouring down his brow, mixing with the downpour.

A woman, also bruised about the face, stood next to the man and Richard. She had black hair, cut short, with straight bangs matted across her forehead, and a wide face. There was a gun in her hand, aimed at the approaching party, and a small pile of gold bricks at her feet.

Moran's air-gun was still aimed at Patricia's back, but it was clear to everyone that a quick shift of a few degrees would be all that was necessary to put a bullet in Jack or Ernie. Carla also had her pistol out and leveled at the supposed poachers.

"Well, well, well," the woman drawled. Her voice was coarse. "Looks like we have a Mexican standoff."

"Patricia," Carla asked, "are these two Jack Hare and Ernie?"

Patricia nodded. A slow burn washed up her neck like the tide rolling in, shading her bronzed skin crimson. Her fists clenched and unclenched. The adrenaline brought on by her deep anger and emotion also served to clear her head somewhat.

"Ernie, short for Ernestine, Belville," the black-haired woman said, "daughter of the second son of Lord Belville, as long as you're asking. And I don't mind telling you a bit, since none of you are leaving here alive. The family's fallen on hard times, and I mean to have this loot Austin owes us."

Ernie cocked her weapon and spoke to Patricia. "You, dearie, I'll shoot out your kneecaps now and then save you for last. I never did get to finish with you."

"Hold it," Carla said. "We can't all start shooting now. The sounds of the shots will carry all the way to Lambton. We don't want to rouse the authorities. There's got to be a way to work this out. We'll split it with you—"

"You may be right," Ernie interrupted. "There is a better way to work this out."

She nodded at Jack. The knife flashed, and a second, and very large, very red mouth split open in Richard Deguy's neck. Blood pumped and gushed out of the gaping wound as Jack pushed Richard's body forward into Patricia and then dived to his right.

Patricia fell backward under the dead-weight and Richard's blood covered her, mingling with rainwater and mud, and soaking her blouse. She rolled to the side to get out from under him. Before she knew it, both she and the body made several revolutions as gravity took over, and they rolled down the hill in a tangle of living and lifeless limbs.

The two came to a rest and Patricia extricated herself from Richard's corpse, shoving it aside on its back. His open, dead eyes stared into oblivion.

She bounced to her feet and looked up the hill in time to see Doctor Moran fire a silent bullet from the air-rifle at Jack Hare.

A red dot blossomed on Jack's forehead, and bits of red and grey brain and bone plastered the old stones of the Tower behind him.

"Thank you, old man," Ernie yelled. She threw a gold bar and caved in Moran's skull. The elderly doctor collapsed on the muddy ground like a marionette, blood running from his cranium in tiny rivulets and draining into the dirt.

Carla, eschewing the moratorium on noisy gunfire, shot at Ernie several times, hitting her once in the shoulder, and causing her to drop her own weapon. Between the continued gunfire from Carla, and the sinister thunderclouds and sheets of rain cloaking the area in darkness, Ernie had no chance of finding and recovering her weapon in the muddy mess. She took off down the hill, headed for the cover of the vast woods.

Patricia realized Ernie bore straight for her and came out of her paralysis. She ran ahead of Ernie. The remains of her tattered and blood-soaked blouse and skirt and stockings tore off in the branches and bushes as she darted through the woods.

Once she was deep enough in the forest that Ernie couldn't see her, she leaped for a high branch, catching it in her right hand. She used the momentum to swing herself around and up to the branch and landed on it, squatting to maintain her balance. She wasn't high enough up; Ernie would see her if she happened to look up when she came barreling by. Patricia launched herself at a higher branch and kept on climbing, then settled into a crook between a branch and the trunk.

Patricia had been through a lot, been drugged and weakened, but she was a big girl, with a fantastic genetic heritage on both her father and mother's sides, a magnificent physique, and a remarkable set of skills, a result of her father's comprehensive physical and mental training program.

In fact, she had been tutored by some of the finest instructors of the day. Violet Holmes had passed on her uncle's techniques of deduction and the whole art of detection, while her parents' friend Benson had taught her knife-throwing and shared his mastery of disguise. Her father frequently took her to the firing range at the New York headquarters of an international enforcement agency associated with the United Nations—Doctor Wildman had been instrumental in co-founding the organization in the mid-1940s—where she trained with two top marksmen, a Canadian and a Russian; she was especially fond of the agents' modified P-38s. She trained in judo with the leather-clad Mrs. Gale; in kung fu with the chauffeur of a prominent Detroit newspaperman; and, with Allard, in the art of blending in with the shadows. From her own mother, she learned breaking and entering, safe-cracking, pick-pocketing, and general thievery. Of course her father was an expert in all of these disciplines, and many more, but he felt it would expand her horizons to learn from others as well.

Most relevant to her current situation, Penelope Gray Smith had trained her to swing through the forest and scamper from tree to tree as if born to the branches, which, in a sense, Mrs. Smith had been, the result of her Kenyan upbringing.

Now, crouched in the tree limbs of the Pemberley forest, Patricia didn't have long to wait. Ernie lumbered through the trees on the path Patricia had just vacated. Patricia held her breath, and Ernie ran past under the tree in which Patricia was hidden.

Patricia was about to jump to the ground and dog Ernie's trail when she heard another cracking of branches from back in the direction of the Tower. Carla burst through the brambles, and ran past Patricia's sanctuary, stalking Ernie.

Patricia decided to stay up higher and track both of the women from above, as long as she could find trees within jumping and swinging range. She was naked, but the rain slicked off her bronze skin and hair. She considered ditching her boots as impractical for branch-hopping. But she had trained with Mrs. Smith both in bare and clad feet, and ultimately decided to keep her boots on in case she ended up back on the ground and there were sharp rocks and pebbles.

She followed the general direction—it would have been generous to call it a path—Ernie and Carla had taken, deeper into the woods. The storm raged now. It was difficult to see and locate anyone, or anything, in the downpour, and Patricia focused her other senses on the pursuit. She would have to be careful. She now cast herself in the role of the huntress, but she knew full well that although Ernie and Carla were after each other, they were also both after Patricia.

Neither could allow Patricia to remain alive.

She continued to hurdle from tree to tree, branch to branch, until she came to a small clearing. She scanned the area and saw a shape, a darker grey in the grey rain, move about fifty feet away, to her right, where another copse of oaks began. She leaped to the ground and sprinted across the clearing, legs and arms pumping and breasts heaving, painfully aware that Carla would have a clean shot at her if she were seen.

Patricia barreled head-on toward the grove, which was bounded by a depression, almost a ditch. Knowing she had too much momentum to stop in time, especially on the rain-slicked grass, she put on an extra burst of speed and hurdled the gap.

She would have made it, too, if the hand hadn't reached up out the blackness, grabbed her ankle, and pulled her down into the dike.

22.

PATRICIA COLLIDED WITH the opposite bank, forcing a great whoosh of air from her belly. She was pulled down into the gully as she scrabbled and scraped in vain for a handhold among the dirt and exposed roots.

Patricia slid to the bottom and landed on her back. The person to whom the hands belonged landed on top of her, straddling her, knees pinning her shoulders, hands pinning her arms. Ernie Belville smiled at Patricia and said, "I'm going to do you sweetie, and then I'm going to kill you." She bent down and kissed Patricia, thrusting her tongue into her mouth.

Patricia bit down, hard, and Ernie screamed and tried to jerk backward. Patricia bit her on the nose for good measure, and Ernie rolled away, crying out and cradling her face in a mass of torn flesh and blood.

Patricia launched to her feet, still breathing hard from her dash across the vale, and spit out the tips of Ernie's tongue and nose.

"You'd better stop wailing," she said. "Keep it up and Carla will find us in no time, and she's the only one with a gun."

"You bith," Ernie said, "I'm gonna futhing kill you…"

"I should kill you for what you did to me."

"You luffed it, you bith, you came—"

Patricia kicked Ernie in the face, sending her sprawling back against the embankment. Ernie cried out in rage and launched at Patricia, tackling her. She bit Patricia on the breast and took out a small chunk of flesh, but fortunately missed the nipple.

Patricia kneed her in the crotch and then punched her in the left shoulder, where Carla's bullet had lodged. Ernie curled up in a ball and howled.

"Be quiet, you idiot," Patricia hissed. She got Ernie from behind and pulled the woman's left arm behind her back, causing a fresh flow of bright blood to discharge from the bullet wound.

"Quiet!" she said again. "Be quiet or I'll snap it."

Ernie whined a bit but was otherwise silent.

"The only way we'll get out of this," Patricia said, "is a truce. We keep on fighting, Carla finds us, bang, we're dead. Understand? No money, no gold. Dead. Got it?"

Ernie nodded, slowly.

"Good. Then I'm going to loosen up on you in a minute. First, promise no more attacks. We get out of here, get to the house, call the police. I know you don't want the police, but it's better than the alternative. Right?"

Ernie nodded again.

"All right, swear then, no tricks."

"I...swear."

Patricia relaxed her hold on Ernie's left arm. Ernie's right elbow slammed into Patricia's gut. Patricia, reacting on instinct, retightened her grip on the left arm and it snapped with a satisfying crack. Ernie elbowed Patricia again and she went down in the mud, clutching her abdomen.

When she regained her senses and looked up again, scant seconds later, Ernie was gone.

Patricia climbed up the bank of the dike and peered over the edge. She saw Ernie disappear into the woods.

Patricia pursued her, only stopping to arm herself by breaking off the longest, straightest, thickest tree branch she could find. The tip of the branch was roughly pointed, which was good since Patricia didn't have the tools or the time to sharpen the branch.

Despite her super-normal vision, she relied also on her other senses. She stopped every twenty feet or so to listen and sniff at the air. She cut almost 90 degrees to the right and started off again at a trot. She thought she must have resembled her relative, the seventh duke and lord of the African jungle, as she raced naked through the Pemberley Woods, perfectly proportioned muscles working under the smooth, bronzed skin.

Patricia stopped again, seeing no sign of Ernie, and then heard a sound from the tree branches above and behind her. She pivoted and planted the makeshift spear on the ground pointing upwards.

Ernie dropped toward Patricia, and then she was impaled as gravity brought her down and the deadly stick was thrust between her legs and up into her abdomen.

Blood boiled out of Ernie's mouth and she tried to move forward, but the stick between her legs hindered her, and she tipped over like a ponderous Martian tripod. She lay in the grime and mud, the torrential rain washing away the blood as it continued to leak out of her dead mouth.

Patricia stumbled backward and sat in the mud next to Ernie. Then she turned to the side and heaved. She was violently sick at the killing. This was the first time she'd killed another human being, but it had been necessary.

And although she remembered her father's policy of humane rehabilitation, she also knew he did end up killing his foes when he had to, or least giving them the chance to avoid falling prey to their own schemes, which they usually failed to do.

Besides…the bitch Ernie had raped her and later tried to kill her.

Ernie got what she deserved and Patricia, despite the brief episode of sickness, had a hard time feeling bad about it.

Patricia heard rustling in the woods and was brought back to reality. Ernie was dead but Carla was still out there, looking for her with intent to kill.

Patricia figured her best advantage was to take back to the trees. If she remembered correctly, this thicket spread nearly to the lake shore on the opposite side of the manor house. She could then swim the lake underwater. From the lake edge closest to the house was a thirty–foot sprint across open ground and flower beds, but it couldn't be helped. It was her best chance of getting to the house undetected. From there she could call the police. She considered whether she should also call Parker for help, and dismissed the idea; she really had no idea where his loyalties were, and for all she knew he could have been in on the plot.

It took her about twenty minutes to make it through the treetops to the edge of the grove, somewhat longer than it might have taken if the torrent hadn't made the branches and trunks treacherous and slippery. She surveyed the surroundings and honed in on a dark shape piled at the lake's edge.

She looked, listened, smelled, but didn't detect anyone nearby. Still, she was cautious. The downpour could dull the effectiveness of even her hyper-attuned senses. In the end, however, she had no choice but to investigate.

She jumped to the ground with the stealth of a leopard and crept toward the pile. She approached and realized it was a body of small stature, dressed in a baby blue bathrobe. Wiry arms and legs covered in black matted hair stuck out of the robe.

Patricia knew it was Austin before she turned him over. But she wasn't expecting to find a small red bullet hole in the center of his brow, just like the third eye Moran's air-gun had made in Jack Hare's forehead.

23.

PATRICIA LOOKED UP to see Carla running toward her, and she took off back into the forest.

Carla still had a gun but she didn't shoot. Patricia assumed this was because Carla still wanted to avoid attracting the attention of the authorities. But if this was so, Carla must not be thinking clearly. There were too many bodies and too much carnage now to cover up anything, and when it was all said and done and the storm lifted, everyone's schemes would come to light.

Carla wasn't thinking of the consequences, though.

Patricia would have preferred to stay to fight. But with Carla brandishing the gun and Patricia not knowing whether or not she planned to use it, running was the better part of valor.

So the chase was on.

Patricia was now even more exhausted after the battle with Ernie. She took to the trees again, back in the direction of the Tower, and then lay in wait. Carla didn't disappoint and passed under Patricia's tree. Patricia leaped, knocking Carla flat.

Patricia put a knee in the small of Carla's back and grabbed her wrist, twisting it. The gun came out of Carla's nerveless hand and Patricia knocked it away into the brambles.

Carla was flexible, however, and kicked up behind her; the heel of her riding boot slammed into the back of Patricia's skull, dazing her. Patricia's body melted to the ground beside Carla.

Carla sat on top of Patricia and began battering her face. Blood spurted from Patricia's nose and ran down her face into her eyes, blinding her. She grasped at Carla, ripping her shirt off and then squeezing one breast in her left hand and twisting it.

Carla screamed in rage and pain and punched Patricia again on the side of the face. Patricia kept on squeezing with one hand, found Carla's throat with the other, and began to apply pressure to her windpipe.

Then, knowing where Carla's head must be based on the throat clenched in her right hand, Patricia let loose of Carla's breast and began pummeling her face with a series of left jabs.

Blood and skin and gore flew. Patricia was much larger and stronger, but she was almost done in after all the drugs she had been given over the past few days, and the combat she had just had with Ernie. And Carla was lithe, sinuous, and agile. In normal circumstances it would have been no contest, but under these conditions Carla was posing Patricia a serious challenge.

Patricia needed to end this, soon, or Carla would outlast her and kill her. Patricia stepped up the beating with her left fist until Carla swayed and her eyes rolled up in her head. She listed to the right like a sinking ship.

Patricia was up and behind her in an instant, holding Carla in a half-nelson, one hand passed under Carla's arm and locked at her neck, her other hand pressing hard against Carla's head.

She squeezed.

"What's it all about, Carla?" Patricia asked. "I know why you want to kill me now, I've seen too much. But why were you and Richard and Moran after me before?"

"I told you, I didn't want to kill you, I wanted us to kill them…"

"Skip it. You've a funny way of showing it. You either wanted to kill me or get me to renounce my claim. I heard the three of you discussing how your grandfather was some kind of Vicomte and a crook, and talking about some kind of proof from the duchess, something to entitle Richard to inherit the dukedom. It'll never work. You and dear departed Richard are her grandchildren only by adoption."

"You're wrong, Patricia. If you died, then the duchess could've passed the estate to us, and the title of the Duke of Greystoke on to her adopted grandson, Richard, by admitting we're her real grandchildren."

"How can that be?"

Carla breathed hard but didn't answer.

Patricia applied pressure to her neck. "Talk, or I'll break it."

"Don't. I'll tell you," Carla said. "Richard and I are really the biological grandchildren of the duchess; she had a child by a man who claimed to be a Vicomte, but he was really a con artist. He called himself Le Comte de Guy. It was during one of the duchess' estrangements from the sixth duke. When they reunited, she couldn't admit the affair, so she said the child was the orphaned son of a couple she had met in Palermo, and that she had adopted him."

"Then your and Richard's father—"

"Carlo Deguy—"

"—was really the duchess' biological son."

"That's right. So we can inherit. But not with you in the way. So we, and the duchess, had to get rid of you, without suspicion, and tried to scare you off. The duchess was relying on the curse—"

"Then she really wasn't part of your plan to kill me?"

"I told you, I'd have rather killed Richard and Moran, and shared everything with you. Screw his title. We still can do it, share the estate, if you renounce—"

"Not a chance. Just tell me if the duchess was in on it."

"She wasn't. Her heart couldn't have taken the strain. And we had to work fast and furious because of the uproar Jack and Ernie were causing; we couldn't keep it from the duchess forever, and the stress might've killed her. So we couldn't delay, because if the duchess died first, her will wouldn't mean a thing, even if you died afterwards. But if you died, or renounced, first, then the estate would have gone to the duchess, who could have then passed it on to her natural grandchildren—Richard and me."

Patricia was quiet for a few moments, digesting the information, but not slackening her hold one iota. Then she said: "I should break your neck."

She didn't have the chance.

A silent bullet pierced Carla's chest, and a fountain of blood bloomed from between her naked breasts. Carla went limp and slid to the ground. Her breath was wheezy and gurgling.

Patricia realized that whoever had Moran's air-gun must be approaching and would be upon them soon. She crouched low behind Carla's body.

"Guess…you won't have to break…my neck now…" Carla said.

"I wouldn't have—"

"I know."

"But you deserve it, for drugging me and taking advantage of me the past two nights."

"What do you mean…?" Carla was fading.

"You, posing as the ghost of Bess to scare me off, drugging me, making love to me."

"I…wouldn't have minded, but it wasn't me…"

Carla died.

24.

ATRICIA REALIZED THAT from a distance and in the gloom, the shooter must have thought there was only one target he (or she) was aiming at. She stayed with Carla's corpse, trying to blend in and make it appear as if there were only one person on the ground, rather than two.

Although, technically, Carla wasn't a person any more.

Doctor Augustus Moran approached the body, air-rifle held casually at his side. There was a large, bloody dent in the side of his head, and Patricia couldn't imagine how he was up and walking around, let alone going on a murder spree with what looked like a hundred-year-old air-gun.

Cursing, Moran now realized Patricia was there too, and began fumbling to reload his one-shot weapon.

Patricia ran off, headed for the Tower, but the old man was after her. She thought about traveling the treetops again and ambushing him, but that scenario wasn't as attractive when her pursuer had a rifle. If he saw her before he came close enough for her to pounce, he'd pick her off easily at a distance.

The Tower was a better option, a level playing field; Moran would have a hard time aiming the air-gun in the twisting and turning corridors.

She made it to the ruins of the Tower, well ahead of Moran, who had fallen behind due to age and his poor physical condition. She ran past the corpses of Richard, with his extra mouth, and Jack Hare, with his extra eye, and dashed in the stone archway entrance. She made two revolutions up the ramp tunnel which curved around the inside circumference of the Tower, and peered out a second story window in time to see Moran creeping in the entrance at the Tower's base.

From the second level, the curving ramp ended and turned into a narrow staircase. Patricia padded up the crumbling stone as quietly as she could, and arrived at the fourth level. She stopped there and ducked in an interior room. The next level up was actually the open-air roof of the Tower, bounded by parapets and ramparts; she didn't want to be trapped there. She planned to wait in the shadows to the side of the doorway and let him pass. Then she would either follow him and ambush him on the roof, or descend quickly, though quietly, and run like hell for Pemberley.

"Miss Wi-ald-maaan," called Moran. "Oh, Miss Wi-ald-maaan. Come out and play, won't you? Won't you come out and play with kindly old Doctor Moran?"

There came a high-pitched whine which lasted almost a minute. When it died, he continued: "Did you hear that, Miss Wildman? Can you guess what that was? No? It was a pneumatic compressor, a nice, modern, portable model. The air-gun's all primed and ready for you now, Miss Wildman. How's that for you, you were running from an old man who didn't even have a shot. But I do now, Miss Wildman, yes I do!"

Patricia held her breath as he approached, continuing to mock and tease her. "I was only knocked out, you know, Baroness. I'm a tough old bastard, yes I am! And after all I've done for her, after all the years, almost fifty years, the old bitch wasn't even going to put me in the will with an equal part after running you off...Just a small sum and free lodging, that's it. But it works out, after all, doesn't it? Nothing to gain from the will, so no one will suspect me; me, kindly old Doctor Moran. Oh, Miss Wildman, I've got the cure for what ails you, I do indeed. Get my hands on that

Robbery money, and live in style, I will. But then poor Austin showed up, must've heard some of the commotion, and I had to shoot him first before chasing you and Carla. Got to kill everyone, you see. And I'll kill the last remaining witness, Miss Wildman, beautiful Miss Wildman, wipe all the prints off the trusty air-gun here, go put it in Miss Belville's cold fingers, rebury the swag, and collapse somewhere in the forest with my caved-in skull. Poor old Doctor Moran, the only survivor of a heinous assault by the poachers. They'll have a devil of a time reconstructing this crime scene, and the dead tell no tales—which means you, my dear Miss Wildman, you, have to die."

Moran passed Patricia's hiding place and she held still. He was still chortling and congratulating himself as he mounted the narrow steps to the roof. Patricia didn't actually think his plan could succeed, but he did make it sound reasonable in his madness. And he was mad. Perhaps it was almost fifty years of abuse from that harridan, the dowager. Or perhaps it was this morning's violent events. Or both. But whatever the reason, he was undoubtedly mad, and that made him more dangerous.

Patricia didn't care. She was tired of being on the defensive. She went up the stairs after him.

The stone stairway opened up to the roof through a hole at one end, and Patricia slowly raised her eyes past ground level, ready to duck and run at the first sign Moran noticed her. He was at the edge of the bulwark, facing away from her.

She crept up further and crested the last step.

Then she slipped and fell on the rain-slicked stone pavers.

Moran whirled. He raised the air-gun stock to his shoulder and aimed it at her forehead.

A figure in motion blurred from the left side of her field of vision. Parker tackled the old man and sent him tumbling, spiraling like a pinwheel, screaming, over the ancient stone blocks of the rampart walls, onto the ground below.

Patricia shook a little but waved Parker off. She leaned over the edge and peered down. Yes, the old man's head really was smashed this time, like a watermelon on a hot summer sidewalk.

She turned around and realized Parker was staring in frank admiration at her nakedness. "Good old Peeping Pete. Getting another eyeful while you can, my friend, just like the other night?"

"Now, Patricia, it wasn't like that, I swear—"

"I know, Pete, I know that now. I just enjoy making you miserable."

"—and besides, you are naked, and for God's sake look at you, I mean, you're beautiful, and that bronze skin, and those big brown eyes, and those weird gold flecks in them—"

"Pete, shut up. Yes, I'm naked. And it's raining. That means I'm cold. Be a gentleman."

Then she allowed Parker to put his jacket around her—it was a few inches shorter than some of her shortest mini-skirts, and thus left some of her tanned bottom exposed—and take her in his arms.

But if he expected tears and sobs, he was going to be disappointed.

25.

ATRICIA AND PARKER arrived back at the estate as the storm broke and the sun's rays flooded in from the east. They climbed the massive grey steps to the terrace and entered Pemberley House through a set of tall French windows letting into an eastern-facing sitting room.

The old duchess reposed on a settee, one twisted hand clutching at the arm of the settee, the other clawing at her heart.

Edith, Duchess of Greystoke, was dead, an expression of horror on her face, and Patricia saw a white apparition fading away.

Patricia swore that Bess must have appeared to the duchess and she died of fright, but Parker laughed. He went to the next room to find a phone and call the police.

Neither of them, of course, was terribly upset over the old lady's death, not, at least, at the moment. But that probably made sense given all the death and violence they had seen this morning.

Besides, she had been an unlikable bitch.

Patricia continued to ruminate on Bess's appearance to the duchess. It made sense the duchess had been fearful of Bess's hauntings, since she was in the actual line of descent from the d'Arcys, as Patricia had learned from the Saxon Blake tale. But Bess only appeared at midnight on the appointed nights. Had Bess come to her, Patricia, last night and then also to the duchess?

If that was the case, then why was old crone dead of fright downstairs in the sitting room instead of upstairs in her bedroom, where she should have been at the midnight hour?

Patricia came to agree with Parker that Bess had not frightened the old dowager to death, although she didn't see eye-to-eye with him on whether or not Bess existed. After all, if it hadn't been Carla in her room every night at midnight, then who, or what rather, had it been?

Of course, Carla could have been lying, to the very end.

But if Bess had not frightened the dowager to death, then the only explanation was that the old lady had heard the shooting outside in the early morning, had come downstairs to find the great house empty, everyone gone, and her heart gave out from the anxiety and worry.

Then Patricia realized and saw what was strange about the ghost, the apparition, she had just seen; it was the duchess herself, not Bess.

And so Pemberley House had a new ghost.

⟶⟫⟫⦅⟵

The police and coroner had come and gone, clearing away all the corpses and the Robbery treasure.

Parker was not what he appeared to be, either. No one in Pemberley House was, it seemed, although, at least, this revelation was a positive one.

Parker explained to Patricia that he was a policeman, planted at the vast estate to keep an eye on the poaching situation. While real poachers were always a concern, the police had also suspected Austin played a part in the Great Train Robbery, and once Doctor Moran had hired him on as the duchess' chauffer, the police placed Parker at Pemberley as a spy.

It turned out that police work and detection were in Parker's blood. His father had been a Scotland Yard inspector, and his maternal uncle, after whom he was named and who called him by the nickname "Peterkin" when he was a very young boy, was an amateur sleuth of some note and fame in the 1920s and '30s. His father's uncle had acted as the amanuensis and partner of a noted consulting detective named Pons.

"I also have a slight confession," he said.

At Patricia's raised brows, he reassured her. "No, nothing untoward, at least, I don't think so. But when I was first assigned to go undercover here, the family names rung a bell and I did a little research. Turns out my mother and uncle's grandmother was Joane Clayton, who was the sister of both the fifth and sixth Dukes of Greystoke."

"What? You're kidding."

"It's true," he said. "Could I really make this up?"

"You mean to tell me that my great-grandfather and your great-grandmother were brother and sister? That we have the same great-great-grandparents? What does that make us?"

"Hell if I know." He grinned. "But distant enough that it doesn't make a difference."

But Patricia wasn't thinking about sex, at least, not at the moment. "Does this mean Pemberley goes to you?"

"No, no, not as I understand it. My descent from the fourth Duke of Greystoke, our great-great-grandfather, was through a female line. The Duchy and estate would not pass through that lineage."

"I need to call Mr. Newell…"

"By all means, but let me reassure you. Since you're descended directly from the sixth duke through a lineage of male heirs, even an illegitimate one—"

"Yes, Mr. Newell said the estate was mine, but that I'd have to apply for a special grant, since the peerage is extinguished, to bestow to me the title Duchess of Greystoke with new letters patent."

"That sounds right. Anyway, call Newell tomorrow and I'm sure he can clear everything up."

"How do you know so much about this, anyway?"

"Ah, in my youth, I dabbled in a bit of writing, and my researches took me on many and varied paths."

In fact, Parker told Patricia, he had been intent on becoming an adventure and crime novelist. Then, almost fifteen years before, he had joined up with an agency called Knight Errant Limited, as an investigator and information-gatherer on-the-scene, in order to gain life experience for writing his novels. Knight Errant had been dedicated to helping those in need, those who had problems the police or ordinary detectives couldn't solve, much like Doc Wildman's and Benson's organizations in the 1930s and '40s. When the firm folded, Parker had missed the excitement and joined the Yard like his father before him.

"Pete," Patricia said the next day, "if you still have a taste for stories, then you'll want to read this one. Maybe then you'll believe me about the ghost of Bess and the curse."

"Why would a story make me believe in ghosts?"

"Because it's not just a story. Every other detail is accurate. The duchess. Moran. This house. The sixth duke. My father, even. And although Richard was a bastard and a liar, I think he was telling me the true legend of the Pemberley Curse, even if he didn't really believe it himself and was only trying to frighten me off. What he told me is exactly what's in this story, in a magazine from the 1920s."

"All right, all right, I'll read it, if only to satisfy you. Where is it?"

She told him of the mystery of the wandering pulp magazine, which had never been satisfactorily explained, and that the prior evening she had found the itinerant periodical and the rest of her missing reading materials neatly stacked on a shelf in the library.

Parker sat on the leather sofa to read the story, and when he got near the end, she joined in reading where she had left off a few days before, when the magazine had disappeared from her room:

> "Ardan [they read] must...make love to the ghost when she appears."
>
> "Excuse me?" Ardan asked, not sure he had heard correctly.
>
> Blake repeated himself.

Ardan had heard him correctly.

He pondered this for a little while, then asked, "Literally or figuratively?"

"Literally."

"That's it." Francis Ardan stood up abruptly. "Your Grace, I apologize. I can't help you, after all. I take my leave of you." He turned to Blake. "I accompanied you on Holmes' word. I can see now I was mistaken to do so. I have seen a few strange things in my time, Mr. Blake, but you're crazy," he said simply, and left.

"Well, Mr. Blake, I tend to agree with my husband's grandson," said the duchess. "I hope you're satisfied with this latest disruption. I, for one, am quite relived he is gone; the reminder of my late husband's illegitimate son was most painful. You have done your damage for the day, now please leave."

"Certainly, Your Grace, my apologies," Blake said, although he privately reflected on her hypocrisy. A quick call to one of Blake's operatives on the Continent, Baron St. John-Orsini, had dug up the duchess' affair with the self-styled "Comte de Guy" and resulting birth of a child in 1909, during another period of estrangement from her husband; the "adopted" Carlo Deguy was doubtlessly her illegitimate son.

Carlo Deguy also would be subject to the curse if he was present at Pemberley. Loathe to further incur the dowager's wrath, Blake rejected the option of bringing Deguy to Pemberley House. He knew the old lady would only deny that Deguy was her natural son, and so raising the issue was pointless.

Holmes had also provided further information on the duchess, most of which was not of immediate bearing, but might prove useful later. All in all, she was not a pleasant sort.

So why, then, was he going out of his way to continue helping this high-handed woman who so clearly did not want his assistance? Well, he reflected, he still had her retainer. That obligated him to earn the whole fee. Besides, the case did have its distinctive touches.

Blake and Topper made haste to depart, and then Blake turned back. "I don't suppose I could use your telephone? No? Then do you know if the Fighting Cock Inn down the road has a public 'phone?"

"Enough!" The duchess stormed out of the hot-house, then turned back and pointed a clawed finger at her secretary. "Moran, see that they leave. Throw them out, if you have to. Now!"

"Yes, duchess," Moran replied with a self-satisfied grin, and produced a small, black semi-automatic pistol.

"Oh, we're leaving, put that thing away before you hurt yourself, old boy," said Blake, swatting at Moran's arm and sending the gun flying into a potted palm.

"Guv'nor!"

"Relax, Topper, the hammer wasn't cocked; our Mr. Moran's not a very experienced thug. C'mon, we'll show ourselves out."

Topper looked back at Moran, who was rubbing his arm where Blake had hit him, then shrugged and ambled after his mentor.

* * *

Over twenty-four hours later, darkness hung over Pemberley House as the midnight hour approached. It was the first night of the three-night cycle which marked the anniversary of Bess d'Arcy's murder at the hands of her husband, over 350 years ago.

Three shadowy figures clad entirely in black silently crossed the gardens, skirted the lake, and approached the massive manor house. Two of the men climbed up to a dark first story window, while the third stood guard below. Cutting tools and suction cups were pulled from black kits; glass was cut and quietly set on the ledge. A black-gloved hand reached inside through the hole and loosened the latch. One of the men entered the great house, while the other remained at the window.

Midnight came and went.

An hour or so later, the third dark figure emerged from house, and both men climbed down from the ledge, joining their companion on the ground.

The three stole away silently.

* * *

Several days later, after the three-night cycle had passed, Saxon Blake presented himself at Pemberley House once more and requested one final audience with Edith, Duchess of Holdernesse.

"Her Grace will see you," Mr. Moran said smugly, as they walked once more down the Great Hall, "but I warn you, she'll not suffer your insolence gladly. She has completely recovered from this ghost story foolishness and there can be no further business between you."

Blake shrugged and said nothing.

When they arrived in the hothouse, Blake immediately requested privacy.

"Duchess, please—!" protested Moran, but she cut him short, responding to a hard glint in Blake's eyes.

"No, Augustus, I think in this case we shall humor Mr. Blake. It shall be the last time, I assure you."

Moran left, clearly reluctant, and Blake sat at a gesture from the duchess. "I'll come straight to the point. Did the ghost of Bess d'Arcy appeared to you on any of the three nights?"

"No. We did have a break-in several nights ago."

"How unfortunate. Nothing was taken, I trust?"

"Nothing. In any event, the matter of the ghost is closed. I'll never tell Augustus, of course, but he was right. There is no ghost. An old lady's folly. I'm sorry I ever called upon you, but please leave, and return no more. You plague me more than Bess ever did."

Blake smiled at that. "But Your Grace, I never returned your retainer and I've earned my fee. You hired me to solve your ghost problem, and it is solved."

"Impudent man!"

"You'll receive my bill for services rendered next week. Unless you'd care to settle up now…?"

"I won't pay you, I swear," she said, with venom. "Why should I?"

He shrugged. "Threat of legal action?"

"There's not a court in the land that'll believe you and your absurd ghost stories. I warn you, those who undertake to intimidate me come to no good end."

"Yes," Blake replied, "perchance I *am* taking my life in my hands. I know what happens to people who blackmail you."

The duchess' eyes narrowed, but she said nothing.

"However, you leave me with little other choice," the detective continued. "Perhaps you recall the circumstances of the infamous blackmailer Charles Augustus Milverton? He was murdered, shot to death, in his home in Appledore Towers in Hampstead, some 28 years ago. His murderer was never identified, although doubtless it was one of the many victims of his pernicious schemes."

A long silence settled over the room.

Then she buzzed for Moran, instructed him to bring her pocketbook, wrote out a cheque for a princely sum, and handed it to Blake.

* * *

The sleuth rejoined the faithful Topper in a waiting taxicab parked outside Pemberley, and the two men headed back for the Castle Hill train station just east of Lambton.

As they departed, Topper asked Blake if he thought the ghost was really gone.

"Of course," Blake replied, "why not?"

"Well," said his plucky apprentice, "we only went to the Pemberley estate one night. The legend has the ghost supposedly appearing for three nights running. Are you sure we shouldn't have gone all three nights to make sure the ghost was well and truly gone?"

"No," said the detective, "the dowager didn't see the ghost any of the three nights. Old Bess is gone, that's for sure. Cheer up, Topper, we solved the case! Now, it's back to Baker Street for us. New clients and cases are already waiting, right? There's a good lad."

Topper nodded earnestly at his mentor, and settled himself in for the short trip to Lambton, and the longer train ride back to London, and home.

But he wasn't entirely assured.

* * *

EPILOGUE

Doctor Francis Ardan—otherwise known as Doctor James Clarke Wildman, Jr.—sat in the cockpit of his modified Ford tri-motor at Croydon Aerodrome, making final checks and cross-checks in preparation for his expedition to the mysterious East, when his superhuman hearing picked up a slight rustle behind him.

Whirling around faster than any normal man had a right to, Ardan confronted the intruder.

"Dad!"

The man formerly called James Wildman came in and seated himself beside his son. "Easy, my boy, easy," he said, holding up a hand. "Your reaction time never fails to astonish me. All the physical, mental, and scientific training I've invested in you has certainly paid off. And will perhaps compensate in some small way for my past wrongs," he added somberly.

"Father," said Ardan, instantly reverting to his usual impassive demeanor, "I didn't know you were in England. For that matter, I thought you could never set foot in England again."

"Yes, son, all too true. However, I was called here on very short notice. Emergency business. My presence here in England is a secret, and I do need to depart immediately before I'm discovered."

The younger man nodded, aware that any further inquiries would be typically stonewalled. Such had it always been between father and son.

"However," the elder man continued, "I couldn't pass up the opportunity to see my son off on this historic expedition. I'm very proud of you, my boy."

"Thank you, sir," said Ardan, nonplussed at this display. "May I at least ask if your business was concluded successfully?"

"Yes," his father replied with an uncharacteristic grin, "yes it was, indeed."

THE END

"You see?" Patricia asked Pete. "Everything fits. The story matches up with the family history, the local geography, Pemberley House, in every way. The legend said if someone can show Bess's ghost love, instead of terror, she will go away. Blake deduced that meant actual physical…affection. My grandfather did it, and the ghost went away."

"But not entirely, according to your own assertions right now, Patricia," Pete responded.

"That's because Blake made a mistake. He only had my grandfather come to Pemberley one night, instead of all three."

"How inconvenient."

"Look, Carla denied entering my room and posing as Bess, and I, in my drugged state, made love to whoever did come to my room at midnight. It could only be the ghost, and besides, she haunts no more."

"Well, I'm still skeptical, Patricia. After all, even if there was a ghost, there's no proof she haunts no more. There won't be until the anniversary next year. And even then, lack of evidence on next year's anniversary won't constitute proof positive that Bess was here this year."

"You're twisting—"

"On top of that, you told me yourself that you only got, as you put it, affectionate with Bess, or whoever it was, on nights two and three. So by your own theory, the ghost will be back, if not next year, then some time."

"But—"

"Also, I have to point out that as the great-great-grandson of the fourth Duke of Greystoke, I'm also lineally descended from the d'Arcys; if I was also subject to this supposed curse, how come I never saw Bess?"

"That's easy. You only joined the household a few weeks ago, and didn't sleep in the main house where Bess appeared. You were never in the house at midnight."

"Well, I was that one night when Miss Neston called me to come see if you were all right."

"That was after midnight, Pete."

"Fine," he said, "we'll let that one go. But here's another point. If Carla and Richard were really the biological grandchildren of the duchess, and the duchess really was a descendant of the d'Arcys, like the Blake story says, then why weren't they ever visited by Bess?"

"Perhaps it's a matter of belief in, or, at least, openness to believing in, the legend? If Richard and Carla never really believed it…"

"Aha! I agree they didn't believe in it, though I don't agree disbelief prevented them from seeing Bess. Now, here's how I see it. Someone close to the family, maybe Moran himself, shared all sorts of private details with some pulp writer, who turned it into a ghost story, a potboiler. It makes more sense that Richard and Carla and Moran used the story to create and hatch their plot to scare you off. And of course it was Carla making the midnight visits to your room, using the secret passageways. You've admitted you were drugged, and she was happy to come shag you; it was obvious how hot she was for you."

"Then why was the duchess scared of Bess? Why did she believe in the curse?"

"Because the ghost story, that fictional Saxon Blake story, was bandied about by Moran and the twins so much she started to believe it herself. Perhaps she had dementia in her old age."

"She was volatile and mercurial, but she was sharp as a tack. But since you have an answer for everything, what about this?"

Patricia retrieved *Excessively Diverted, Or, Leaving Pemberley* from its shelf and showed it to Parker. "This is an account by Delhi Darcy, the daughter of Fitzwilliam Bennet Darcy. In it, she complains that the reason her father sold Pemberley to Sir Gawain wasn't financial reverses; in fact, the family continued to live in great comfort—just not at Pemberley. Delhi's mother Agatha, however, insisted they vacate the house when her father began to anticipate with too much pleasure the annual visits of a certain ghost."

"The fantasies of a teenager," Parker responded, "upset at being uprooted from the only home she's ever known. In fact, Delhi's little ghost fantasy probably gave Moran the idea to devise the Blake tale. Patricia, there are no such things as ghosts."

"Then why did this…this person who came to me in my room so dramatically resemble the portrait of Bess that's hanging in the Great Hall?"

"Again, you were drugged, and suggestible. And you yourself have remarked on Carla's resemblance to the portrait, which makes sense if she was a distant descendent of the d'Arcys. A change of hair and some makeup was all that was needed."

"Damn it, Pete, I know what I saw, and felt, and the ghost of Bess was real. You're impossible, a rationalist, just like my father."

Parker smiled. "I'll take that as a compliment. Besides, if I'm to write mysteries, I'd better be able to solve them."

"Write mysteries? I thought you were focused on real, not fictional, police work now."

"You inspire me, Patricia. Perhaps I'll take up the pen again." He pulled her toward him and kissed her.

Patricia responded, and the two silently agreed to table the discussion of Bess's ghost.

They moved to the Kodiak bear rug on the floor in front of the fireplace and made love, and Patricia didn't think of her father once.

Epilogue

SIX MONTHS HAD passed.
The larger section of Pemberley House was still open for public historical tours, but a plaque at the gates to Pemberley House informed visitors that the other side of the estate, accessible by a private drive, housed the firm Empire State Investigations.

Lady Wildman and Parker were in her private suite. She had decided to take Bess's room on a permanent basis, and had expanded it into a master suite by knocking down a wall and combining it with the room next door.

They had just killed half a bottle of champagne—Veuve Clicquot, her mother's favorite—and gone to bed.

Parker was lying on his back and Patricia had just lowered herself onto him, moving back and forth rhythmically, enjoying each other and the moment.

The red phone on the side table next to the bed rang. Parker objected but Patricia reached over, carefully keeping him still inside her, and picked up the phone. The red phone was a private hotline, not the firm's public line. When someone called it, it was on matters of vital importance.

"Empire State Investigations."

"Lady Patricia Wildman, please." The voice was a woman's, thin and nasal.

"Speaking. Who is this?"

"You have long-distance call, via radiophone. Would you like to accept the charges?"

"That depends. Who's calling?"

"Hold please." Patricia could imagine the operator at the other end. Grey-hair in a bun, microphone and earphone clamped to her head, sensible shoes and spectacles, sitting among row upon row of identical, nasal-voiced women at banks of grey metal consoles.

"What's going on?" Parker asked. "I've got a serious case of—"

"Shush. Don't know, I'm on hold. Sounds like an international call."

"How's that? I thought only the Prime Minster and M had this number—"

"Shhh—"

The nasally operator was back. "I need to confirm you are Lady Patricia Wildman, Baroness of Lambton?"

"I said it was. I asked you who was calling me before I accept the charges. This is a highly secure line, no one should have this number."

"Hold please."

Patricia growled in frustration.

"Mmm, that felt good, do it again," Parker said.

"What?"

"When you growled. It squeezed, just so, and—"

The operator returned and Patricia shushed him. "Lady Wildman, the caller will not identify himself. Will you accept the call?"

"Yes, fine, I'll take the bloody call, put it through."

"Thank you, connecting you now."

The line crackled as the signal echoed through the ether. Then came a voice. It was a rich and mellifluous voice, deep and reassuring, although rendered eerie and hollow by the great distance separating the speakers.

Most of all, the voice was familiar, and one Patricia had never thought to hear again.

"Patricia, this is your father."

Editor's Notes

1   That is, the man calling himself the seventh duke, William Cecil Arthur Clayton, apparently died in late 1972 at age eighty-one. The real William Cecil Arthur Clayton died in 1910. He was the "William Cecil Clayton," the cousin of the Jungle Lord, seen in Edgar Rice Burroughs' novels *Tarzan of the Apes* and *The Return of Tarzan*. Upon William Cecil Clayton's death, John Clayton (the Lord of the Jungle) was legitimately entitled to become the eighth duke of Greystoke; however, he so resembled his late cousin that he decided instead to adopt his cousin's identity, in order to avoid the inevitable publicity which would accompany the revelation that an English lord, a peer of the realm, was a feral child raised in the wilds of Africa by "apes." Farmer knew this, or deduced this, based on his "An Exclusive Interview with 'Lord Greystoke'" which took place on September 1, 1970, or else from the extensive research which formed the basis of his biography, *Tarzan Alive: A Definitive Biography of Lord Greystoke*. Or both. Lord Greystoke persuaded Mr. Farmer to suppress certain details, such as his impersonation of his late cousin. From 1910 until 1972, when Greystoke faked his death and that of his wife, he refused to see his late cousin's mother, the dowager duchess, since she was the only person still living who could easily penetrate the impersonation. The "death"

of the Jungle Lord—the ostensible seventh duke of Greystoke—in 1972, leaving no other heirs, left Patricia Wildman as next in line of succession to inherit Pemberley House and the associated estate. When, in 1974, a lost manuscript by Doctor John H. Watson, *The Adventure of the Peerless Peer*, was released and revealed that Sherlock Holmes had discovered the impersonation in 1916, the Jungle Lord, acting through a series of trusted middlemen, used his influence to have the book suppressed. Farmer, who edited the Watson manuscript for publication, received a friendly warning letter from Greystoke, now residing in parts unknown under an assumed name. (Farmer was not surprised at receiving the letter, since Greystoke had indicated in their 1970 interview that he would soon fake his death and disappear.) The Lord of the Jungle was also aware that Farmer, in the course of interviewing Patricia Wildman for the biography of her father, Doctor James Clarke Wildman, Jr. (first published in 1973 under the title *Doc Savage: His Apocalyptic Life*) had learned of Patricia's adventure in England when she came to investigate the Pemberley estates. In the event that Farmer decided to publish Patricia Wildman's story, Greystoke strongly encouraged him to alter and fictionalize any details about Greystoke's impersonation of the seventh duke. Obviously Farmer intended to comply, although he never ended up completing Patricia's story. Very shortly thereafter, in late 1974, Greystoke reversed himself on the issue of the impersonation; he freely admitted to the deception in memoirs which he provided to Farmer ("Extracts from the Memoirs of 'Lord Greystoke,'" *Mother was a Lovely Beast*, Philip José Farmer, ed., 1974; *Tarzan Alive*, Bison Books, 2006). It can hardly matter, some thirty-five years later, if the truth about Greystoke's impersonation is noted here, especially in light of the fact that the Jungle Lord was not entirely successful in suppressing *Peerless Peer*, back in 1974; that he himself admitted it in his Memoirs; and that he has apparently approved of its recent republication in the collection *Venus on the Half-Shell and Others* (Christopher Paul Carey, ed., Subterranean Press, 2008). It should also be mentioned that more recent editions of Burke's *Peerage* now reflect the correct information:

"Sir William Cecil Arthur, seventh Duke, b. 18 May, 1891, educ. Eton, Cambridge, d. unm. 1910, in Gabon, the marquessate of Exminster, the viscountcy of Passmore, and the baronetcy becoming extinct according to the limitations of heirs male of the body, and was s. by his cousin, John Clayton, eighth and present Duke, who was discovered alive in Gabon, having been raised after the death of his parents by the aborigines."

2   The Dowager Duchess of Greystoke (Edith Jansenius) still being alive in 1973, at age 103, contradicts Philip José Farmer's *Tarzan Alive: A Definitive Biography of Lord Greystoke*; Farmer quotes Burke's *Peerage* as citing her death in June 1907. The mystery behind the error in Burke's remains unsolved.

3   As we now know, this is not technically true. The fifth duke's son, John Clayton, and his pregnant wife Alice Rutherford Clayton were lost at sea when the *Fuwalda* went down off the shores of the island of St. Helena in 1888. However, John Clayton and his wife survived on the coast of French Congo for several more months, into the year 1889; they lived one day past the date of the fifth duke's death. Their son, John Clayton, was later immortalized in Edgar Rice Burroughs' *Tarzan of the Apes*. As noted earlier, after the death of William Cecil Clayton, the seventh Duke of Greystoke, his cousin John Clayton (the Lord of the Jungle) was legitimately the eighth Duke of Greystoke; the Jungle Lord adopted his late cousin's identity and became the seventh duke in order to avoid publicity.

4   The Jungle Lord took pains to keep the existence of his children—natural and adopted—hidden from the world-at-large. He didn't care about passing on his titles to them and they had all the income they needed from the gold reserves he had found and preserved at a prehistoric hidden city, an outpost of the ancient African empire of Khokarsa. He even carried the deception forward in his "Extracts from the Memoirs of 'Lord Greystoke'" which indicated that his natural son Jackie had died in infancy.

This contradicted the information Farmer had discovered and presented in *Tarzan Alive*, namely that the natural son, John Paul "Jackie" Clayton had indeed lived, married Alice Horatia, and had a son of his own in 1943. Greystoke lied in his "Memoirs" to muddy the waters and protect his family from unwanted investigation in the wake of the publication of *Tarzan Alive*. Farmer felt partially responsible and agreed to be complicit in publishing some of the untruths or half-truths in the "Memoirs" to help the ape-man and his family cover their tracks. Which is not to say that everything in Greystoke's Memoirs is false; far from it, most of it is true, but key pieces are misdirection. In any event, given the lengths Greystoke had gone to conceal knowledge of his children, and grandchildren, from the world-at-large, he could hardly leave them to the public's eye after he faked his and his wife's deaths. In fact, *Tarzan Alive*, which Farmer wrote in 1970-71, indicated that Greystoke was then planning to arrange a false death for himself, Jane, John Paul (the biological son), John Drummond-Clayton (the adopted son), and Drummond-Clayton's wife Meriem. "Young John Armand [the son of Drummond-Clayton and Meriem] would then become the ninth duke of 'Greystoke.'" John Armand would arrange his own faked death at a later time.

However, it's not hard to postulate that upon the 1972 publication of *Tarzan Alive* and the resultant attention, the family amended the plans and agreed that John Armand would join the rest of the family in faking their deaths and taking new identities. They had all the wealth they needed and no need to maintain their interest in the peerage, which in some ways was a liability as a driver of unwanted attention—unwanted, because all the family members had access to and were using an anti-aging elixir Greystoke had discovered. The Jungle Lord and his family, as they made the decision to have John Armand also fake his death, did not realize this would cause the extinction of the Greystoke peerage, but if they had it wouldn't have changed their decision. As it happened, nearly simultaneous with the faked deaths of Greystoke and family came the very real, tragic, and mysterious death of Sir Beowulf William Clayton, Bt. Sir

Beowulf was the great-grandson of Sir William Clayton, who was the younger brother of the fourth duke of Greystoke. Upon the mass "extinction" of the Jungle Lord, his sons, and grandsons, the Greystoke title would have passed to Sir Beowulf, but for his untimely and unexplained death. It is fortunate that Sir Beowulf translated approximately one-third of a particular diary and, just before he died, furnished it and a set of notes to Philip José Farmer which enabled Farmer to reconstruct the true story behind Jules Verne's *Around the World in Eighty Days*. Farmer titled his account *The Other Log of Phileas Fogg*. Sir Beowulf left no sons, and the Greystoke title went extinct.